WHEN
THE DOLLS WOKE

Look for these and other Apple Paperbacks in your local bookstore!

The Dollhouse Murders
   by Betty Ren Wright
Me and Katie (the Pest)
   by Ann M. Martin
The Ghosts Who Went to School
   by Judith Spearing
Veronica the Show-off
   by Nancy K. Robinson
The Trolley Car Family
   by Eleanor Clymer
Cassie Bowen Takes Witch Lessons
   by Anna Grossnickle Hines

WHEN THE DOLLS WOKE

THE

Marjorie Filley Stover

Pictures by Karen Loccisano

AN
APPLE
PAPERBACK

SCHOLASTIC INC.
New York Toronto London Auckland Sydney

For Carissa, Sean, and Shelley

ISBN 0-590-44624-X

12 11 10 9 8 7 6 5 4 3   1 2 3 4 5/9

Printed in the U.S.A.   28

First Scholastic printing, December 1987

Contents

WURLING FAMILY TREE

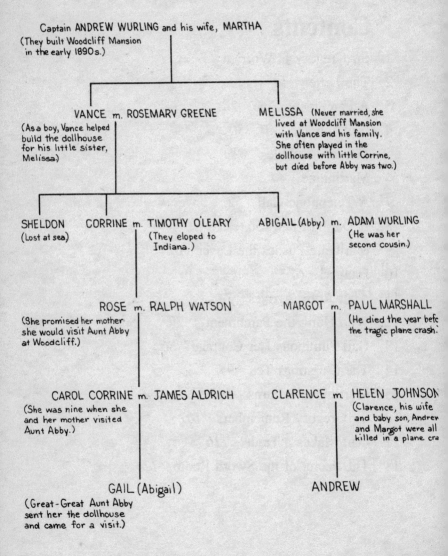

Captain ANDREW WURLING and his wife, MARTHA
(They built Woodcliff Mansion in the early 1890s.)

VANCE m. ROSEMARV GREENE
(As a boy, Vance helped build the dollhouse for his little sister, Melissa.)

MELISSA (Never married, she lived at Woodcliff Mansion with Vance and his family. She often played in the dollhouse with little Corrine, but died before Abby was two.)

SHELDON
(Lost at sea)

CORRINE m. TIMOTHY O'LEARY
(They eloped to Indiana.)

ABIGAIL (Abby) m. ADAM WURLING
(He was her second cousin.)

ROSE m. RALPH WATSON
(She promised her mother she would visit Aunt Abby at Woodcliff.)

MARGOT m. PAUL MARSHALL
(He died the year befc the tragic plane crash.)

CAROL CORRINE m. JAMES ALDRICH
(She was nine when she and her mother visited Aunt Abby.)

CLARENCE m. HELEN JOHNSON
(Clarence, his wife and baby son, Andrew and Margot were all killed in a plane cra

GAIL (Abigail)
(Great-Great Aunt Abby sent her the dollhouse and came for a visit.)

ANDREW

1
Sir Gregory Is Worried

The dollhouse stood shabby and neglected in the playroom at Woodcliff Mansion. Once it had been very grand, with its four stories, gleaming white pillars, tall red chimneys, and elegant furnishings. Now it had a raggedy-taggedy look. The pillars were dingy and the chimneys crooked. Wallpaper curled down at the corners, cotton stuffing poked through a hole in the sofa, and a chair tipped crazily on a broken leg. Dust was everywhere.

Woodcliff, too, wore an air of neglect. The house had been built in the early 1850s when fast Yankee clipper ships sailing in and out of Boston Harbor had made the Wurling family fortune. That was long ago. Today both family and fortune had almost disappeared. Only Abigail, the last of the Wurlings, was left in the old home. She was nearing ninety.

In the dollhouse, Sir Gregory sat stiff and unmoving, deep in sleep at the big oak desk in the Sword Room. This was a large room on the ground floor. Its walls were paneled with pine. A huge fireplace built of pink, irregular-shaped pebbles stretched across one end. Two dusty steel swords crossed each other above the mantel.

At the sound of voices and a tapping of feet, Sir Gregory woke. *The children are coming,* he thought. He wondered sleepily, *Which children?* The clear vapors inside his hollow china head stirred. It had been months since anyone had opened the playroom door.

It was not the children, after all. Sir Gregory could not see the visitors' faces, but he could see three pairs of shoes. He had had a great deal of experience observing shoes. These belonged to three women.

First there was a pair of shiny black shoes; next came gray alligator shoes, not new, but expensive-looking; and last a pair of low-heeled brown shoes. Sir Gregory listened to the voices with growing alarm. Black Shoes wanted to buy the dollhouse.

Buy the dollhouse! Sir Gregory was wide awake now. His vapors began to churn. *This is our house! It belongs to us! It has always belonged to us, and we belong to Woodcliff Mansion.* Sir Gregory knew. He had been there from the beginning.

Brown Shoes pointed her feet straight at Black Shoes.

"You're a dealer in antiques, Mrs. Harper. I work at the Children's Museum. We both know the dollhouse is worth more than that."

"Look how shabby it is," retorted Black Shoes.

Sir Gregory bristled. *Shabby! That's not our fault. We try our best.*

His wife, Lady Alice, often fretted and fussed. "What we need is a little girl to fix up our house—to make new drapes and polish the teapot. Then we could have parties with real tea in the pot, fancy cookies, and company."

The doll children, Maribelle and Tommy, loved parties—especially the cookies. Even Baby Winky in her cradle was given a cookie at parties.

What we need is a little girl to love us and play with us, Sir Gregory tried to tell the owners of the black, brown, and gray shoes.

No one heard him.

"I agree that the dollhouse needs fixing up," Brown Shoes answered Black Shoes. "It needs fresh wallpaper and paint and new drapes, but it was well built by a cabinetmaker who knew his business."

Sir Gregory nodded to himself. *Built by old Jed, the master carpenter, and young Vance Wurling.* It had been Vance's idea—as a birthday present for his little lame sister,

Melissa. She was enchanted with it, and Vance had offered to build more furniture.

The voices were still bickering. "The Children's Museum would also like to buy the dollhouse," continued Brown Shoes. "Unfortunately, we can't afford to pay what it's really worth. I've been wondering, Mrs. Wurling," the pleasant voice hesitated, "if you might consider making a gift of the dollhouse to the museum in memory of your daughter, Margot."

The museum? Give our house to the museum? Outwardly Sir Gregory was stiff and composed, as always. Inwardly his vapors swirled faster. *What about us? We don't want to live in a museum. We don't want to move away.* With all his might he began to wish, *Stay with the Wurlings. Stay with the Wurlings.*

All this time the person wearing the gray alligator shoes had not spoken. Now the gray shoes twitched, and an old voice quavered, "That's a lovely idea, Anne."

"I'll double my offer," snapped Black Shoes.

Gray Shoes sighed unhappily. "I need the money. Need it badly. However, when I said the toys were for sale, I wasn't thinking of the dollhouse."

Sir Gregory's vapors whirled. In spite of the quaver, he knew that voice. *Abby! Abby grown old the way real people do!* Of all the little girls who had played in the dollhouse, Abby had been his favorite. Now she was in trouble.

The old voice was wistful. "You and my daughter Margot were such good friends, Anne. You spent many happy hours playing in the dollhouse. I know that you really care, but I don't think Sir Gregory would be happy in a museum."

"Sir Gregory not happy!" exclaimed Black Shoes.

Old Abigail tried to explain. "Sir Gregory is the adventurous type. He'd feel cooped up in a museum. Besides, the dollhouse must stay in the family. I promised the Captain a long time ago."

Promised the Captain! Sir Gregory felt a tingle down his china backbone. A memory bubble floated up through the twirling vapors. He saw the swaying light of a lantern and a man's heavy boots in front of the dollhouse. A face weathered by salty spray and tropic suns peered into the Sword Room. He recognized Captain Vance Wurling.

What a night that had been! Crammed into a corner, Sir Gregory could not see exactly what was happening, but he remembered the scratching and the scraping noises. He remembered, too, when the Captain held him in his great hand. "You'll not give away the secret, will you, Mate?" the Captain demanded. Sir Gregory promised; but there had been more. *What else had the Captain said?*

The memory bubble burst as Black Shoes sniffed in annoyance. "Your father was a sea captain. Why should he care what happened to a dollhouse? You need the money, Mrs. Wurling. Sell the dollhouse to me."

Brown Shoes' voice was gentle. "You want the dollhouse to stay in the family? But Mrs. Wurling, you no longer have a family. That's why I thought of the museum."

The gray shoes shifted. "There's little Abigail."

"Little Abigail?" Black Shoes and Brown Shoes asked together.

"Yes, my sister Corrine's great-granddaughter. I've never seen her, but she was named for me."

"I'd forgotten you had an older sister," Anne of the brown shoes said. "That was long before my time, although I think Margot did tell me once. Didn't Corrine elope and move west?"

"Yes, she and her husband went west, all the way to Indiana," said the old voice. "As a child I was the one who wanted excitement and adventure, but I've lived in Boston all my life. I married my second cousin, Adam Wurling, and did not even change my last name."

The gray shoes shuffled restlessly. "The dollhouse would make a lovely memorial to Margot. Still, I need every penny I can scrape up. Yet, I promised the Captain . . ."

"You must do what you think best," Brown Shoes told her.

The gray shoes planted themselves firmly. "A promise is a promise. I shall send the dollhouse to my namesake, Abigail Aldrich."

The vapors tossed wildly in the hollow pit of Sir Gregory's china body. The dolls had wished for a little girl to fix up their home, but they had expected her to come to them, not for them to go to her. Where was this place called Indiana? What kind of a little girl was Abigail Aldrich?

Sir Gregory was worried. But dolls were never asked what they wanted or did not want to do. He was thankful for his stiff china backbone.

2
The Letter

Gail Aldrich bent her head against the December wind. Her red-gold hair whipped about her cheeks, and she pulled her blue stocking cap tighter. But it was not the chill wind that brought the scowl to her face.

If only Susan could have moved, too! Until two weeks ago, she and Susan had lived in the same apartment house. They had played together, gone to school together, and shared their secrets. That was before Gail's parents had unexpectedly bought a house on the other side of town. Now Gail and Susan did not even go to the same school.

She was walking home from the Bensons, where she stayed after school until Mother and Daddy returned from work. Three-year-old Betsy Benson was chubby and cute and fun to play with, but Betsy was no help making friends at school. Susan would have been acquainted with everyone by the end of the first day, thought Gail glumly. She had not realized how much she depended on Susan.

"You'll soon make new friends," Mother told Gail, but Gail had not. Always shy, without Susan she felt as strange as if she had lost an arm or a leg.

Gail shivered at the memory of that awful first day. Mother had taken her to the school office. After a few words with Miss Thompson, the principal, Mother hurried off to work. Miss Thompson was friendly and smiling, but she had no time to talk. She handed Gail an admittance slip and asked a boy passing in the hall to show her Mrs. Hardy's fourth-grade room.

Gail entered timidly, her eyes nervously searching out the teacher. She did not see long-legged Pete Anderson's outstretched foot. She stumbled and fell against him. There were lots of giggles. Gail, her face tomato-red, made her way to Mrs. Hardy's desk.

When Mrs. Hardy asked her name, she stammered, "G-G-Gail Aldrich—that is—I mean, Abigail Aldrich, only I'm always called Gail." She clutched at the blue beads that had been Susan's parting gift.

The class tittered again. Mrs. Hardy rapped for order and pointed to an empty seat. Gail sank into it, embarrassed and angry. She hated this school. She hated everyone in the class. Eyes on her desk, she failed to see that a dark-haired girl turned around to give a friendly smile.

She'd show them, Gail vowed silently. She knew she could beat them all in arithmetic. However, when Gail bested green-eyed Madge in a multiplication contest, Madge muttered, "Think you're smart, don't you?" and several children giggled.

"Good for you," the dark-haired girl had whispered. Gail, grasping the blue beads, had not looked up.

If only Susan lived next door, Gail thought again as she turned in at an old-fashioned house with gingerbread trim and a wide front porch. She glanced up at her room on the second floor. The round tower at the corner with its cone-shaped roof made her think of a castle.

Gail stopped at the mailbox and pulled out a magazine and several letters.

Not until Mother and Daddy were ready for their coffee did Daddy sort through the letters that Gail had placed in a neat pile on the dinner table. He flipped an envelope to Mother. "Here's one from your Great-Aunt Abby."

Mother shook her head sadly as she slit open the envelope. "Poor Aunt Abby—all alone since that terrible plane crash two years ago. To think they were going to visit her. Her daughter, Margot; Margot's son, Clarence; and his wife and their baby son—all gone in the blink of an eye!"

Gail let a spoonful of peppermint ice cream melt on her tongue and tried to decide whether to telephone Susan after supper. She longed to talk to her, but already Susan had a new best friend. It wasn't much fun listening to Susan chatter about what a good time she and Pam were having. Gail only half-listened as Mother began to read aloud.

"'Dear Grand-Niece: No doubt you will be surprised to hear that I have decided to sell Woodcliff Mansion and go into a retirement home.'"

Gail looked up at Mother's cry of dismay. Mother had wanted to visit Aunt Abby last summer. She was disappointed when Aunt Abby wrote that she had already made plans to stay with friends on Nantucket Island in August. Gail and her parents had gone as usual to Grandfather Aldrich's cottage on Lake Michigan.

Mother read on. "'I can no longer afford the upkeep, taxes are high, and the house is too big for one person. My faithful Mandy and Sam are going to live with their daughter, but they are helping me sort and pack.'" Mother shook her head sadly. "Poor Aunt Abby." She turned the page and gave an excited gasp. "Listen to this! 'I have decided to send the dollhouse to your little Abigail.'"

"To me!" Gail's cheeks turned peppermint pink. "She's sending the dollhouse to me?"

Mother laughed. "After all, your great-grandmother Corrine was Aunt Abigail's sister. It was her dollhouse, too."

Daddy let out a low whistle. "We bought this house just in time. There wouldn't have been room in our little apartment for a big dollhouse."

"Aunt Abby says, 'It needs a bit of fixing up, but Corrine and I had such happy times playing in it that I can't bear to think of giving it to strangers. Anyway, a long time ago I promised my father I wouldn't.'"

"Why would it have made any difference to the old Captain?" asked Daddy. "Why should he have cared?"

Mother shook her head. "I can't imagine. Of course, he helped build it and took an interest in it for years."

"From all reports, he was a queer old fellow. And isn't Aunt Abby nearly ninety?" asked Daddy. "Maybe her mind wanders now and then."

Gail leaned forward, her red-gold hair gleaming in the lamplight. "Tell me every single thing you can remember about the dollhouse," she begged.

Mother looked dreamily into space. "It's a very old dollhouse. It was old when I was a little girl. Of course, I only played with it that one week when my mother and I visited

Aunt Abby in Boston. My mother died when I was twelve, so I never went back. It was the grandest dollhouse I've ever seen. It was filled with tiny treasures that Captain Vance Wurling had found on his voyages around the world." Mother's voice dropped to a whisper. "Sometimes I felt as if the dolls were really talking to me."

Gail's eyes shone like blue stars. Her ice cream melted into a pink puddle, forgotten.

3
A Parchment Clue

Sir Gregory lay still in his tissue paper wrappings. The bumping and jostling and the screeching and pounding had stopped. He did not think it was the noise that had wakened him.

No, it had been something else. The clear vapor in his hollow head had been stirred by a familiar signal—a signal pulsing on the air waves in much the same way that a radio station sends sounds through the air. The signal was the presence of people. It had not been a strong signal, but it had been enough to rouse him.

He hoped Lady Alice had not wakened. She was so easily frightened.

Sir Gregory often told himself that he could not have found a more beautiful wife if he had chosen her himself. To be sure, Lady Alice cared nothing about exploring. She preferred pretty clothes and parties to exciting adventures, but he saw nothing unusual in that. They made a handsome couple, and Sir Gregory could balance a teacup on his knee as readily as he could scale a cliff.

He was also proud of their three children, Maribelle, Tommy, and Baby Winky. He was glad that they would always stay the same. They never outgrew their clothes or had to have their tonsils out the way real children did. He and Lady Alice would never grow gray-haired and wrinkled. There were many advantages to being a doll.

Their greatest peril was that being made of bisque (a kind of unglazed china), they were breakable. He himself had once broken a leg while on an adventure with little Abby. She had been more upset than he was until her sister Corrine glued his leg back together. The scars would always be there, but his trousers hid them, and he did not limp.

A whisper interrupted Sir Gregory's thoughts. Lady Alice, lying beside him in her tissue paper wrappings, had wakened after all. "Where are we?"

Sir Gregory answered comfortingly, "I think we have arrived. I think we are in Indiana."

"Oh, Sir Gregory," Lady Alice said, trembling, "I'm so thankful you are here." Although they had been married for more than a century, she still called him "Sir Gregory."

"Don't worry your pretty head," he soothed. "All will be well."

"Do you think the new children will be rough? Like Clarence was?" quavered Lady Alice, remembering Abby's grandson. "He cut off some of Tommy's hair, and it will never grow back."

Lady Alice was always imagining the worst. Hurriedly Sir Gregory reassured her. "There's a little girl. I heard them say so."

"I hope she will be like Corrine. Corrine made beautiful clothes, and we gave elegant parties. Queen Victoria came." Lady Alice sighed wistfully. "Life was never the same after Corrine went away."

Sir Gregory did not want to hurt Lady Alice's feelings. However, he had secretly been bored by Corrine's endless parties. It had been Abby who decided that Sir Gregory should be an explorer. Off they would go to hunt for hidden treasures. Now that was the life! However, he answered cheerfully. "This will be a kind little girl who will love and understand us. I feel it all the way up my china backbone."

Gail sat on the living room floor and stared at the dollhouse. Daddy had brought the hammer and chisel and uncrated the big box where the delivery men had set it down.

The dollhouse had a slate-gray roof, red chimneys, and glass windows. It was open-fronted except for double carved doors that opened into the central hallway. Six pillars made of half rounds graced the main front of the house and hid the edges of the walls that divided the rooms.

The house had been built in two sections. The top part consisted of the first and second floors and the attic. The bottom section was one story high. Because it was several inches wider than the top part, it formed a roofless porch, or runway, outside the first floor.

The dollhouse was just the way Mother had described it, except, "It's so raggedy-taggedy looking," Gail said in a small voice. The once-white pillars rising grandly from the first floor to the top of the second were dingy and gray. The wallpaper was stained and peeling. A window was broken, and the draperies were torn and faded.

Gail had been in a dither of excitement when she and Mother began unwrapping the furnishings carefully packed in each room. Now she shook her head sadly. Yellowed cotton stuffing poked through a split in the gold-and-red-striped satin sofa. The red velvet upholstered chairs had hardly any fuzz left.

Mother frowned at a wing chair with a broken leg. "Someone has been very rough. Perhaps it was Clarence."

The brass bowls and candlesticks were tarnished. The harp in the music room had lost all its strings, and the dining table was scratched. Upstairs a pink-flowered water pitcher had a broken handle, and the china washbowl was cracked. Bedspreads were worn and faded. A woolen coverlet was full of moth holes.

"It's so raggedy-taggedy looking," Gail repeated.

Mother shook her head in dismay. "It's going to take more than 'a bit of fixing up.' It will take a great deal of work, and I don't have much time."

Gail nodded soberly. Mother never had time for extras—not since she had gone to work in Mr. Easterday's law office. "But if I hadn't gone back to work," she told Gail once again, "we couldn't have bought this house. We'd still be living in that crowded little apartment with no yard for you to play in."

Gail clutched her blue beads. "I would still have had Susan," she thought. She looked at the walnut stairway curving up to the second floor. There was no stairway to the attic, only a hole with a hinged trapdoor. Like most other attics, this one was stuffed with odds and ends: discarded furniture, trunks, and boxes tied with string.

Gail bent down for a better look at the ground floor. The rooms were paneled in pine, but the windows were only painted.

"The ground floor was not part of the original house," explained Mother. "Aunt Abby said that it was added afterwards to raise up the dollhouse and make it easier for lame Melissa to play in. Turning the ground floor space into rooms was Corrine's idea later. The bedrooms at either end are for the servants, and the big hall in the center is called the Sword Room."

Gail gazed at the wide fireplace in the Sword Room. It was built of pink stones, weathered smooth. Some had flecks of mica that sparkled in the light. A black kettle hung from an iron crane. Two steel swords crossed each other against the chimney. At the top of the wall, a wide molding bore a carved inscription:

THE GREATEST FORTRESS WAS BUILT
ONE STONE AT A TIME.

Gail read it aloud and looked up with a puzzled frown. "What a queer saying to put in a dollhouse."

"The Wurlings came from England. That was their family motto," said Mother.

"In the days of knights in armor, England had lots of stone fortresses," added Daddy. "It was a good motto then and still is. It means that great deeds are accomplished bit by bit."

Gail reached for a framed parchment hanging above the mantel. It was hand-lettered in fine black print. Squinting, she read aloud:

> Forget thee not
>   The Wurling name,
> Nor motto that brings
>   Wealth and fame.
> Build stone by stone,
>   Our motto dear.
> Keep faith and seek
>   Thy fortune here.

"Fortune!" Gail's voice shook with excitement. "Is there a fortune hidden in the dollhouse?"

"Oh, Gail, you couldn't hide a fortune in a dollhouse," said Mother, laughing.

"The verse says, 'Keep faith and seek thy fortune here,'" Gail insisted. "It sounds like a clue."

Daddy smiled. "Your imagination is running wild," he

said. "You could hardly hide a twenty-dollar gold piece in a dollhouse."

"Maybe it was a doll fortune," said Mother. "I remember hearing that when Aunt Abby was a little girl, she was always pretending to hunt for hidden treasures."

"What about your grandmother Corrine?" demanded Gail.

"She liked to sew and give dollhouse parties. She was eight years older than Abby, but she often played with her, and she sewed for the dolls up to the day she eloped."

"Tell me about when she eloped," begged Gail.

"You know the story, Gail," protested Mother. "Corrine fell in love with the stableboy, dashing Timothy O'Leary. Her father was at sea, and her mother warned that she must get his permission to marry. Corrine had always been the Captain's favorite and able to get her way with him. His ship was due any time, and she went right ahead planning her wedding."

Gail shook her head sadly. "But Captain Vance said no."

Mother nodded. "He was furious. His beautiful daughter marry a stableboy? Never! The young couple eloped, and the Captain never forgave them."

"Poor Corrine," sighed Gail. "She never went home or saw her family again."

"It was an ill-fated year," mused Mother. "Corrine's

mother had a stroke. She died after word came that their son Sheldon had gone down with his ship in a storm. They say Captain Vance changed after that. In time, he became somewhat addled and did and said such queer things."

"But Corrine managed to write to her little sister, Abby," prompted Gail.

"Yes, now and then she sent a letter through a friend. Before my Grandmother Corrine died, she made my mother promise that she would visit Aunt Abby at Woodcliff Mansion. I was nine years old when my mother kept that promise. It was then that I played with the dollhouse. Aunt Abby urged us to come again, but Mother died three years later. I never went back."

Gail stared at the raggedy-taggedy dollhouse. "Poor dolls. I wonder what they thought about all those happenings."

Mother reached for a box in the attic labeled "Dollhouse Family." She smiled as she handed the box to Gail. "Oh, I'm sure it didn't make any difference to the dolls."

But Mother was wrong.

4
Gail Has the Gift

Sir Gregory could hear the sound of voices, but shut up in the box with all the tissue paper wrappings, he could not make out what was being said. At last, with a scrabbling of tissue paper, the wrappings were pulled away. A child with red-gold hair stared down at him. He stared back. Corrine's hair had been the same pale red-gold.

"Gail, meet Sir Gregory," he heard a grown-up voice say.

A frown appeared between the girl's blue eyes. "Mother! Look at the holes in his clothes!"

Sir Gregory felt his vapors swirl. He had once been very proud of his dark swallow-tailed coat, his vest, and his gray pinstripe trousers. For some time now, however, Lady Alice had been fussing about those holes. Lady Alice was always fussing about something.

Once Sir Gregory had answered jokingly, "It isn't as if Queen Victoria were coming to tea." Indeed, it had been years since there had been any company. Perhaps his remark was the reason Lady Alice had been upset for a whole week.

"What a pity!" the grown-up voice exclaimed. "Moths have eaten holes in his woolen suit."

"Maybe we could make a new suit," suggested Gail.

The vapor twirled merrily in Sir Gregory's head. *I knew it!* he exulted. *I knew she would be a thoughtful, kind little girl.*

"Christmas will soon be here," replied the grown-up voice. "There are cards to write, presents to buy, and cookies to bake. Maybe we can make the dolls' clothes later."

"Oh, Mother, you'll never have time," groaned Gail.

She is right. Grown-ups seldom have time for dolls, Sir Gregory told himself. *I shall have to wear my suit with the holes.* He wished he could get a better look around, but Gail had laid him on the living room floor, where he stared up at the ceiling.

"That's Lady Alice," the grown-up voice was saying. "Isn't she beautiful? Notice the tiny, even stitches in her blue silk dress."

A thin vapor of pride curled upward in Lady Alice. She had always been proud of her delicate features and elegant appearance. The blue dress was made of silk imported from Japan by a Wurling sea captain. The bodice had tiny tucks, and the long skirt swept over her painted black slippers.

Gail turned Lady Alice in her hand. "But Mother, her hair is all matted, and her dress has a rip and grease spots."

The thin curl of pride collapsed. Lady Alice knew that her hair was matted and her dress ripped, but it was not polite of Gail to say so to her face. *It's not my fault,* she thought bitterly. *Besides, it's up to you to fix me.* Furthermore, why should Gail be so critical when she was dressed so strangely herself? The girl was actually wearing pants like a boy—faded blue pants with a plain white knit top. Not a ribbon or a ruffle in sight. Lady Alice's vapors churned in an angry froth.

Perhaps Gail sensed her anger. Abruptly she put Lady Alice on the floor next to Sir Gregory.

You're wrong, Sir Gregory, hissed Lady Alice. *Gail's hair may be the color of Corrine's, but she does not understand us.*

Sir Gregory did not answer. It was useless to argue when Lady Alice was in this kind of a mood.

Gail turned Maribelle slowly in her hand. The rumpled

pink dress hung almost to the doll's china ankles. A faded pink ribbon was tied around frizzy yellow hair that had once curled prettily over her shoulders. Nevertheless, her dimpled face smiled happily. "She's cute, but her dress is too long," said Gail.

"That's how little girls used to wear their dresses," answered Mother.

Tommy's clothes were old-fashioned, too. His navy blue trousers buttoned onto a soiled white shirt with ruffles down the front. He had a tiny chip on one hand, and someone had snipped off patches of his brown hair.

"Dear me!" exclaimed Mother. "Someone has tried to give him a haircut."

That stupid Clarence! shouted Tommy, but Gail did not hear.

Gail cupped Winky in the palm of her hand. The baby was scarcely an inch and a half long. Her hair and eyes were only painted on, but her arms and legs moved. "How sweet!" crooned Gail, smoothing the long, white dress. She did not put Winky on the floor, but laid her in the walnut cradle in the nursery. With one finger she set it rocking gently.

"That's Becky, the housekeeper," Mother said as Gail unwrapped the last doll.

Becky knew that she was not in the same class with the bisque dolls. She was only a common little rag doll stuffed with cotton. Her eyes, nose, and mouth were embroidered on a plain muslin face. Strands of yellow yarn hair stuck out from beneath a ruffled white cap.

Corrine had found Becky at a county fair in a basket with a dozen other small rag dolls. They had all been made by the chirpy old lady selling them, and except for the color of their dresses and hair, they looked very much alike.

"Lady Alice needs a better housekeeper," Corrine had said, eyeing the basket. "Martinique tries, but after all, Martinique is a foreigner. She has never understood our ways."

This was quite true. Martinique *was* different. Her face was sharply whittled from dark brown wood. She wore gaudy clothes and glass beads and earrings. Sometimes she talked to herself in a language the other dolls did not understand. Captain Vance had brought her from the French island of Martinique in the West Indies when his sister, lame Melissa, was mistress of the dollhouse.

Martinique could do anything that the little girl imagined she could do, and Melissa had taught her to cook very well. Sir Gregory often praised her clam chowder, baked beans, Boston brown bread, and lemon sponge cake. Still, she never quite seemed to fit into the family. There was something queer about Martinique.

Corrine had given the chirpy lady a silver dime and chosen Becky with her blue print dress, white apron, and extra-wide smile. It was extra-wide because the little lady had chanced to take an extra stitch in the curve of Becky's mouth.

Becky was a capable, motherly soul, as good-natured as her wide smile. She had never dreamed of living in such an elegant house. She admired Lady Alice and loved the children. Maribelle, Tommy, and the baby adored her. Becky was an excellent housekeeper. She soon set Martinique to scouring the pots and carrying out the ashes. Martinique was no longer allowed to cook, and she was disgruntled. One day when Sir Gregory had gone exploring with Abby, she disappeared. Everyone was relieved.

Gail grinned at Becky's broad smile. "She looks so happy."

Mother nodded. "The dollhouse family wouldn't know what to do without Becky."

Sir Gregory wholeheartedly agreed. Suddenly, he stiffened. The ceiling was blotted out by a furry black head. Two yellow eyes glistened, and long white whiskers quivered as a pink nose sniffed closer and closer.

Lady Alice gave a horrified gasp. Maribelle choked back a fearful screak. It was a terrifying moment, but Sir Gregory kept his cool. In his adventures as an explorer, he had picked up a great deal of useful information. *Don't be frightened*, he soothed. *The cat can't eat us.*

He's sniffing in a very threatening way, said Lady Alice, trembling.

The only time we need fear the cat is when we move about, Sir Gregory said. *Cats have sharp claws and will pounce on anything that moves.*

At that moment Gail looked down at them. "Gwib, you silly cat, dolls aren't good to eat."

Lady Alice was still nervous. *Why doesn't Gail put us in our house?*

Becky had not said a word although the cat's sharp claws could have ripped her cloth body to shreds. *Let's wish for Gail to move us into the house*, she suggested.

An excellent idea, praised Sir Gregory. *We must all wish as hard as we can.*

Much good wishing will do! sniffed Lady Alice, *unless Gail has the gift.*

Gail had found a tiny bottle in the cradle. She was feeding Winky when she felt little prickles across the back of her neck. Putting up a hand to rub them, she noticed the dolls on the floor. "You want to get settled in your house! Moving is such a job. Becky, you can work in the kitchen. Maribelle and Tommy, you need to straighten your rooms." Gail picked up the dolls as she spoke.

I knew it! Sir Gregory whispered to Lady Alice. *Gail has the gift. If we wish hard enough, she will know what we are telling her.*

Pure luck! insisted Lady Alice as Gail whisked her away.

Sir Gregory paid no attention. He felt in his china bones that he was right.

5
Memory Bubbles

The dollhouse had been placed in the round tower that jutted from the corner of Gail's bedroom. Sir Gregory sat at the oak desk in the Sword Room and shuffled the papers in front of him. He wished he knew what he was supposed to be doing.

"Such a big house, but no study," Gail had said. "Maybe you can work at the desk in the Sword Room." She had taken scrap paper from Daddy's wastebasket and cut doll-house-sized paper from the blank margins. On some of the pieces she scribbled wavy lines to look like writing.

What am I supposed to be writing? Sir Gregory puzzled. *Is it a list of goods for the Wurling warehouses? Is it a secret message? Or is it a contract drawn up by a lawyer?*

Through the years each little girl who played in the dollhouse had had her own ideas about what the dolls were doing. Since the dolls always did what the children imagined, their lives changed accordingly.

Melissa had put Sir Gregory in charge of the Wurling warehouses where their ship cargoes were stored. "You didn't make him a ship's captain?" her brother Vance asked in surprise.

"No," answered Melissa. "Lady Alice would be too lonesome if Sir Gregory went to sea for months and months. Oh, Vance, I wish you didn't have to go. I'll miss you so."

He patted her head. "Our steamships are very fast. When I come home, I'll bring a surprise for the dollhouse."

Through the years Vance never forgot this promise. He brought beautiful miniatures, mere trifles, and quaint dolls from faraway places. When he was grown and married, he still hunted for things for the dollhouse to bring back to his daughters, Corrine and Abigail.

Corrine adored her handsome father in his captain's uniform. "We are a sailing family, and Sir Gregory is a ship's captain," she decided. She made him a uniform trimmed with gold braid. A few years later, to please little Abby, Corrine made Sir Gregory an explorer's suit.

Abby and Sir Gregory climbed steep mountains. They dug for buried treasure, and they carried secret messages.

All by himself, Sir Gregory sailed a ship across a wide ocean. Abby tucked a scribbled paper into the waistband of his trousers where the wind could not blow it away.

"We must get this secret message to Marblehead," Abby whispered. "I'm giving you one half, and I'll keep the other. If I go by land and you go by sea, we'll outwit the enemy. Be careful, and meet me in Marblehead without fail."

Sir Gregory did not know where Marblehead was, and he had no compass. However, Abby gave the clipper a shove, and a strong wind caught the white sails. It blew the boat far out across the water.

Propped against the mast, Sir Gregory watched the shoreline recede. He wished Abby had faced him about so he could see where he was going. He felt the wind in his face, and the ship skimmed over the water like a white bird. When it touched shore, Abby was there, just as she had promised, so he knew he had landed at Marblehead. She was full of praise for his bravery and seamanship.

"I have been to sea, and I was captain of my ship," he told Lady Alice when he returned home.

"Queen Victoria came to tea, and you missed her," said Lady Alice. Sir Gregory did not care. Queen Victoria had come to tea before, but he had never sailed a ship across the ocean.

He did not hear Abby's brother scold her. Sheldon was very cross. "Never touch my clipper ship again! I spent months making it, and you might have sunk it in the pond!"

When Abby's daughter, Margot, was mistress of the dollhouse, Sir Gregory no longer went exploring. He was a lawyer just like Margot's father, Adam Wurling.

Now Sir Gregory was puzzling over the papers on the oak desk. He eyed the books Gail had brought from the parlor. "For your research," she had said.

Research? What kind of research? Am I working on a law brief? Or am I figuring out clues for a secret treasure? Abby and I were clever at finding treasures. But Gail had not heard him.

Sir Gregory felt a tingle down his backbone. A memory bubble floated up, a happy memory of an afternoon when he and Abby had gone hunting for pirates' gold.

"Come with us," Abby had urged Corrine, who sat on a cushion by the dollhouse, sewing. "It's too nice to stay inside."

Corrine shook her head. "I must finish this dress for Lady Alice before I go away."

"Go away?" asked Abby.

Corrine flushed. "Just over to Sarah's house. I'm spending the night with Sarah."

That was the last time I saw Corrine, Sir Gregory reflected. The following afternoon Abby had rushed into the playroom. "Oh, Sir Gregory! Something terrible has happened! Corrine has run away with Timothy O'Leary. They are married and on their way west. Father is in a rage, and Mother is crying. I don't know where Sheldon is, and I don't know what to do." With a sob she clutched him to her. "Oh, Sir Gregory, what am I to do?"

The memory bubbles frothed and foamed. Once again he saw that dark night when the Captain clenched him in his big fist. "You'll not give away the secret, will you, Mate? Swear you'll forget this night until Abby needs your help."

I swear, promised Sir Gregory. Outside the dogs barked. He did not know if the Captain heard him.

Sir Gregory wished he knew exactly what he had sworn to forget. How was he supposed to help Abby? The Captain had not said. *I am a man of my word*, Sir Gregory told himself.

So much had happened after that night that Sir Gregory felt a bit muddled. He had never been good at keeping track of dates. "Never a calendar in the dollhouse," he would complain.

Had it been the next day or many weeks later when Abby slipped into the playroom and slumped in front of the dollhouse? She had taken Sir Gregory from his easy chair in the parlor, and together they had stolen quietly down the stairs. "Mama is sick, and we mustn't make any noise," she whispered.

They headed for Abby's favorite hideout, made by three great boulders, and crawled into the hole. She looked at Sir Gregory, her blue eyes brimming with tears. "Nothing is right since Corrine ran away with Tim O'Leary. Papa won't even let me speak her name. Mama is sick, and Papa won't leave her. Papa's ship sailed this morning with Sheldon aboard."

A bell clanged, and the memory bubble burst. Sir Gregory pushed back his chair. The brass bell that hung outside the front door was ringing. It was intended for guests, but the dolls used it as a dinner bell. As Sir Gregory jumped to his feet, the title of a book on the table caught his eye: *Pirate Gold*. Abby had made the book long ago.

6
Martinique

Lady Alice stood in front of the stove. She was wearing a white handkerchief Gail had folded in a triangle and tied around her waist. "If you wear an apron when you cook, Lady Alice, you won't get grease spots on your dress."

Cook! Lady Alice was thrown into a tizzy. *I'm the lady of the house, not the cook! Becky does the cooking.*

Gail did not hear. She would have been surprised to know that Lady Alice rarely set foot in the kitchen. Gail's mother always did the cooking—unless the family went out to eat or Daddy made chili.

"We'll have tomato soup this noon," Gail had said. She stood Lady Alice by the stove and set a copper saucepan on the burner with a spoon for stirring. "We'll eat in the kitchen to save time." That's what Gail's mother always said.

Eat in the kitchen! If Lady Alice had not been leaning against the stove, she would have swooned. Only servants ate in the kitchen!

Gail reached for the plates on the shelf. "The baby is too little to eat at the table, so that makes five."

Five? Count again. Sir Gregory, Maribelle, Tommy, and I make four. As for Becky . . . Becky makes five! Lady Alice felt as if her head would split.

A few minutes later, Gail's mother called her to help make cookies, and Gail had not played in the dollhouse since. So now Lady Alice stood at the stove stirring the soup. Like it or not, each day they all sat down in the kitchen to eat tomato soup. Then, having completed the pattern Gail had set, they were free to go their own ways.

"To think I should come to this," lamented Lady Alice.

Sir Gregory tried to cheer her. "My dear, the soup is excellent. After all, you can do anything that Gail imagines you can do."

"That's the trouble," wailed Lady Alice. "I don't want to be a cook. And Gail might at least have imagined something like creamed chicken on hot biscuits with peas. For dessert, baked custard with whipped cream and a dab of currant jelly." Her spoon clattered against the bowl. "But no! Like it or not, we have tomato soup."

"Times have changed, my dear," reminded Sir Gregory.

"I liked the old ways better," Lady Alice said stubbornly. "I never did any housework, and we never ate in the kitchen. Melissa was very good at imagining what we needed. Then Captain Vance brought Martinique from the West Indies."

Becky padded into the kitchen and tucked Winky into the high chair. "I wonder if we'll ever know what happened to Martinique. It was strange that nobody saw her go."

For a moment there was silence. Then Tommy said slowly, "I saw her leave. Corrine took her away."

"Tommy!" Becky was vexed. "If you knew, why didn't you tell us when we missed her?"

"I was scared, and I thought she might come back."

Maribelle nodded in agreement. Martinique's tales had frightened them both.

Melissa had begun it by innocently asking Martinique to tell the children a story. Melissa was going to have her tell about Goldilocks and the Three Bears, but just then she was called to supper. So Martinique had told about palm trees and a bamboo hut with a thatched roof; about an old woman stirring a kettle over an open fire; and about dancing and drums beating. She discovered that she liked telling stories. After that, she lured Maribelle and Tommy to the kitchen with cookies and told them voodoo tales.

No one knew that the man who had carved Martinique had uttered strange, secret words over her and planned to keep her for himself. By mistake she ended up in a batch of carvings that his brother carried to market. She was delivered to a little shop owned by a man who sold wood carvings. When business was slow, he and a crony gossiped together for hours about voodoo. Martinique had listened and remembered.

"If you wear claws of lion, you grow strong as king of beasts," Martinique intoned as they sat near the Sword Room fireplace. "Feathers of eagle make you swift with keen eyesight." Martinique had never seen a lion or an eagle, but the shopkeeper had sworn it was so.

Voodoo could be used to cause accidents and harm enemies. To cast a spell on someone, you first must get something which belonged to that person. A lock of hair, a fingernail paring, or a drop of blood were best, but a scrap of clothing or an object the person had touched would do. Even footprints could be used. Sharp stones driven into a man's footprints could make him go home.

Maribelle and Tommy shivered as Martinique droned, "Shopkeeper and friend put spell on man who not do what they want. Make little clay figure and friend cut piece of hair from man's head while he sleep. Then press hair into clay head and speak strange words over it. Next day man slip and crack head on rock. Then he willing to do what they want."

Martinique's tales became more and more frightening. Maribelle and Tommy tried to stay out of her way, but they seemed unable to resist that skinny, beckoning hand. ". . . And boy see voodoo circle scratched in dirt," moaned Martinique. "Boy terrified and not want to step inside. He afraid if he do he turn into chicken or goat. He try to hold back, but feet take him forward." There was a long, quivering wail, and Maribelle and Tommy clung to one another.

"Now boy stand on edge of circle."

"Martinique!" a cross voice interrupted. All three jumped. How long had Lady Alice been standing in the kitchen doorway? "Martinique! Never let me hear you talk like that again! Come along, children. Your father wants us all to go for a walk."

Right after that incident, Becky had come to live with them. The voodoo tales stopped. But in spite of themselves, Maribelle and Tommy sometimes found themselves drawn to the Sword Room where Martinique sat by the fireplace mumbling to herself. When she asked them to fetch something, it seemed safer to do as she asked than risk angering her.

Now Tommy spoke up boldly. "Not even Martinique's voodoo saved her."

"There's no such thing as voodoo spells," Sir Gregory said.

"Martinique used them," insisted Tommy. "I was scared not to do what she wanted."

"I was scared, too," Maribelle said. "She told me to bring a red-gold hair from Corrine's head. When I found one on the floor, Martinique snatched it and dropped it in the kettle."

"She asked me to bring her a chicken feather," Tommy told them. "That very day when Abby was tossing a pillow around on the window seat, a feather flew out! Martinique made it fly out, and she stuck it in the black kettle."

"Stuff and nonsense," muttered Sir Gregory.

Lady Alice leaned forward. "Why was Corrine angry at Martinique? Why did she take her away?"

Tommy slurped a spoonful of soup. "Martinique and I were in the Sword Room and Corrine was sitting on a cushion by the dollhouse, sewing. Martinique stared with her spooky eyes at Corrine until she pricked her finger with a needle, and a drop of blood came out."

Tommy darted a glance at Lady Alice, half-expecting her to shush him. "I could feel Martinique willing Corrine to scrape the blood off on the edge of the kettle so it would roll inside. Only her voodoo didn't work. Corrine grabbed her and wiped her finger on Martinique's skirt. 'Leave me alone! I'll do as I please!' Corrine shouted and snatched her out of the dollhouse. That was the last I saw of Martinique."

"You should have told me right away," scolded Sir Gregory.

"I'm not afraid anymore," said Tommy. "Not even Martinique can find us here in Indiana."

Lady Alice swayed in her chair. "Why? Why did Martinique want a chicken feather, Corrine's hair, and a drop of blood?"

Becky looked up from her soup. "One day she asked me to get a bit of beeswax from Corrine's workbasket. I obliged her. Then I asked what she was making, and she looked right through me with those spooky eyes. 'A charm,' she croaked. 'Now go tend your own kettle of fish.' She could make you feel jittery."

"What kind of a charm was she making?" puzzled Lady Alice. "Why would she want to harm Corrine?"

"Stuff and nonsense," repeated Sir Gregory. He was greatly annoyed to think he had known nothing about these happenings. "Look in the black kettle, and you'll see it's empty."

"Of course it's empty," replied Becky. "Margot cleaned out the kettle years ago. Margot and Anne always kept the dollhouse neat as a pin. I wouldn't have touched that kettle for love or money."

Sir Gregory hardly heard her. He had just remembered that dark night when the Captain had sneaked up to the playroom. Captain Vance had used the black kettle.

7
A Telephone Call

It was Saturday. Gail squatted in front of the dollhouse, the parchment in her hand.

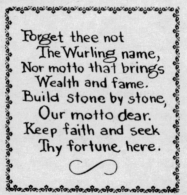

Forget thee not
The Wurling name,
Nor motto that brings
Wealth and fame.
Build stone by stone,
Our motto dear.
Keep faith and seek
Thy fortune here.

Gail read the last two lines twice. She looked the fireplace over stone by stone. Some of the stones were flecked with tiny bits of mica that sparkled in the light. All were firmly cemented in place. Maybe Daddy was right. She was letting her imagination run wild. Gail cocked her head at Sir Gregory. "Do you know the secret? Did someone hide a fortune in the dollhouse?"

Sir Gregory's gray eyes were calm and clear, but the vapors eddied inside his hollow bisque head. *A fortune?* He and Abby had often gone treasure hunting, but never in the dollhouse.

Gail heard Mother's footsteps hurrying up the stairs.

"Gail, Jim! You'll never guess who just telephoned!" Mother's voice trilled with excitement. She stopped outside the study door where Daddy was working.

Gail popped out of her room, but Mother did not wait for guesses.

"It was Aunt Abby, and she's coming to spend Christmas with us!"

"Aunt Abby! Coming for Christmas!" Gail glanced toward the dollhouse. She saw again the peeling paper, the shabby upholstery, and the tattered curtains. "Oh, Mother! We haven't even started to fix up the dollhouse."

Mother waved her hands helplessly. "There hasn't been time. I'm sure Aunt Abby will understand."

"How strange," mused Daddy. "All these years she's never even suggested coming to visit us."

"She had expected to spend the holidays with a friend," explained Mother. "However, her friend has decided to visit her daughter in St. Louis. Aunt Abby can't get into the retirement home yet, and she's eager to get acquainted with Gail."

"Can't get into the retirement home?" Daddy appeared in the doorway. "How long does she plan to stay?"

Mother shook her head. "She didn't say. She asked if it would be convenient, and I told her we'd love to have her come. Why?"

Daddy glanced around the study that doubled as a guest room. "I want her to come, of course, but what if she stays a month, or two months? Sometimes people have a long wait to get into a retirement home."

"We're her nearest relatives now," said Mother. "If she needs help, we must help her."

"You're right, of course," agreed Daddy. "It's just that I had planned to get a lot of writing done during vacation while there aren't any classes. However, I can make do on a card table in our bedroom."

Gail listened in dismay. Daddy's writing was important. College professors were expected to write articles and books. She couldn't help wishing, though, that Aunt Abby could stay for a long visit. She had never known either one of her grandmothers.

Gail went back to the dollhouse. She saw Sir Gregory

sitting at the oak desk, his papers spread in front of him. In a flash she rushed to the study. "I know, Daddy, I know! You could fix up a place in the basement to write. Just like Sir Gregory did in the Sword Room."

"Just like Sir Gregory?" Daddy's eyebrows shot up. "That's not a bad idea, Gail. There's plenty of room in the basement." He grinned. "I've been wishing I had more space for bookcases and a big table where I could spread my papers. It would have to be makeshift, but it would do."

"Then it won't matter how long Aunt Abby stays," Gail pointed out gleefully.

"I could make curtains for the basement windows," offered Mother. "We might find a rug on sale after Christmas." She smiled at Gail. "We can do it a little at a time, building stone by stone as the Wurling motto says."

"Sir Gregory gave me the idea," said Gail. She squatted down by the Sword Room and looked at the parchment again. "Keep faith and seek thy fortune here." When Aunt Abby arrived, she would ask her if there really was a secret hiding place.

8
A Daring Plan

Sir Gregory dipped his spoon in his tomato soup and looked across the table at Lady Alice. The ends of the handkerchief apron stuck up in back like two little white wings. She was staring at her soup. Tommy was eating with noisy gusto, but Lady Alice had not reminded him to stop slurping.

Sir Gregory tried to cheer her. "My dear, I overheard Gail say that they put up their Christmas tree this evening." Lady Alice had always delighted in the Christmas festivities.

Instead of being cheered, she broke into a wail. "Do you suppose we'll have tomato soup for Christmas dinner?"

Sir Gregory groaned inwardly. He had put his foot in it.

"When I think of the Christmases we used to have," sighed Lady Alice. "The house decorated, a Christmas tree in the parlor, and a lovely Christmas Tea with all our friends invited: Queen Victoria, Senorita Lolita, Juan Carlos, Miss Blossom and Miss Cherry . . ."

"Come, come, Lady Alice," Sir Gregory interrupted. "We've celebrated Christmas by ourselves for years now."

"I was hoping that the new little girl would have a Christmas party." Lady Alice dabbed at her nose with her lace handkerchief. "At Woodcliff Mansion you could at least get the toy tree from the cupboard. Here we have nothing. We might as well forget Christmas."

"No Christmas!" cried Maribelle.

"We have to have Christmas!" shouted Tommy.

"The tree decorations are packed in a box in the attic," Sir Gregory reminded them.

"The plaster-of-Paris food is in the attic, too," said Becky. "There's turkey, cranberry sauce, and plum pudding."

"It's too dangerous to pile a table and chairs under the trapdoor and climb up," objected Lady Alice. "Last year Sir Gregory almost fell and broke his leg."

The vapors in Sir Gregory's head whirled faster. "I have it! I'll cut a branch off the Christmas tree downstairs."

It was a daring idea. They stared at him, and Lady Alice's white apron wings shook in alarm. "You don't know your way," she said. "Besides, there's the cat!"

"Boo to the cat!" Sir Gregory jumped to his feet. Hadn't he once sailed across the ocean all by himself?

"Hooray!" Tommy yelled. "I'm coming, too!"

"Me, too!" cried Maribelle.

"No, children," protested Lady Alice.

Sir Gregory soothed her. "Don't worry. They'll be safe."

Lady Alice stood up. "Then I'm coming, too."

Sir Gregory halted in dismay. "My dear, you've never liked to explore." He tried to be tactful. "Stay here where it's comfortable, and Becky can make you a cup of tea."

Lady Alice was stubborn. "If you insist on taking the children into danger, I shall come, too."

He tried to hide his annoyance. "There is no danger. Even if there were, what could you do to help?"

"I can be the lookout," she replied. "While you are getting the tree, I will keep watch for the cat."

Sir Gregory did not have time to argue. "Fall in, anyone who's coming." He strode out of the house with Tommy and Maribelle close at his heels. Lady Alice trailed behind. She swished down the steps, holding her long skirt high to keep from tripping.

"Wait a minute!" Sir Gregory darted into the Sword Room and shoved a stool to the fireplace. He climbed up and with a quick leap landed on the wide mantel.

"Careful!" shrieked Lady Alice.

Clinging to the stones with one hand, Sir Gregory lifted down a sword.

Tommy jigged with excitement. "Is that to fight the cat?"

"I doubt if we so much as see a hair of the cat. We need this to cut down the tree." He marched off, brandishing the sword over his head.

The door of Gail's room was ajar. One by one they slipped through the crack and down the dimly lighted hall. At the head of the stairs, Sir Gregory held out his arms like a traffic policeman. Along one side of the dark staircase a smooth baseboard slanted down. The rounded spindles supporting the handrail made a kind of protecting fence.

"I'll go down first." Sir Gregory seated himself on the baseboard.

"No! It's not safe!" gasped Lady Alice.

Sir Gregory tried to be patient. "Perfectly safe. Just keep your feet pointed straight ahead."

"Sir Gregory, if you think that I . . ."

"Don't fret, my dear. You don't have to come. Tommy, you're next, but wait until I give the signal."

WHIZZZ. He disappeared into the black pit. Moments later, his voice floated up. "All's clear. Remember, keep your toes pointed straight ahead."

"Wheee!" Tommy whizzed down, and Maribelle followed.

"Wait for me!" Lady Alice's voice was shaky but determined.

The three waiting at the bottom saw her disappear into the shadows, but there was no sudden swish. Nothing.

"Where are you?" Sir Gregory was more annoyed than anxious.

"Don't hurry me." Lady Alice appeared in the gloom, clutching the edge of the slide and inching her way along.

"Let go," urged Tommy.

Now that the bottom was in sight, Lady Alice slid the rest of the way. "I knew I could do it," she said triumphantly.

"Bravo!" Sir Gregory held out a hand. "Now, I have a few words of caution—in case we should be separated."

"Separated!" Lady Alice caught her breath.

"Most unlikely," he assured her. "However, Dimwitty's book on exploring advises being ready for any emergency. First, if we should be separated, each one is to make his or her own way back to the stairs and up as fast as possible."

"How do we get back up?" asked Maribelle.

"By sliding up backwards, of course. Use your hands and feet to push. You'll get the knack in no time."

"I knew we should never have come," moaned Lady Alice.

Sir Gregory pretended not to hear. "Second, keep your eye out for landmarks. Third, I am the leader. If I give an order, you must obey at once." He raised the sword on high. "Ready? Follow me."

9
Maribelle Pushes the Lever

Sir Gregory, Lady Alice, Maribelle, and Tommy stood in the doorway gazing at the Christmas tree in the Aldriches' bay window. The drapes had not been pulled, and the glow from a streetlamp glinted on tinsel, golden chains, and bright-colored balls.

"Oh!" breathed Maribelle.

"Ooh!" whistled Tommy.

"Beautiful!" sighed Lady Alice.

Sir Gregory was glad that she had come after all. "Remember," he cautioned, "stick to cover if you can." He led the way, dodging around chair legs, end tables, and a long sofa. Then they crossed a wide open space.

They had nearly reached the tree when Lady Alice uttered a cry of alarm. "Stop! Don't step in the magic circles!" She pointed at three bands of silvery metal circling the tree.

Sir Gregory hesitated. "Don't tell me these are voodoo circles!" he scoffed. Nevertheless, instead of crossing the circles, he followed them around.

"Voodoo is nothing to fool with," warned Lady Alice. Maribelle and Tommy shrank back. Martinique had spoken of voodoo circles drawn in the dust. Anyone who dared step inside might turn into a chicken—or a goat.

Sir Gregory gave a shout. "These aren't voodoo circles! These are railroad tracks, and here is the train!"

Tommy and Maribelle raced after him. They saw a black engine half-hidden in the shadows. Directly behind it was an empty, small open car. Behind that were three cars painted red; all had rows of windows on each side.

"The little car is the tender, or coal car, and the red cars are the passenger coaches," explained Sir Gregory.

"The doors are so small. How do we get in?" wondered Tommy.

"That's why I rode in the tender," said Sir Gregory.

"You?" Lady Alice was amazed. "When did you ride on a train?"

"A long time ago when Abby took me visiting."

"Visiting?" Lady Alice sounded jealous. "Why didn't Abby take me? I'm the one who likes parties."

"Abby and I were going exploring, but her mother took

her calling instead, and she stuck me in her pocket. The two boys at that house had a toy train. It wound up with a key and ran around the track."

"Like the key that wound up Sheldon's tin policeman and made him walk?" asked Maribelle.

Sir Gregory nodded. "The engine had a spring inside and went round and round the track so fast it almost made me dizzy."

"I want to ride in the tender!" cried Tommy.

"No indeed!" scolded Lady Alice. "You might get hurt."

Maribelle peeked under the engine. "Where's the key?"

Sir Gregory shook his head. "This train isn't exactly like the one I rode on. It's probably a newer model."

Sir Gregory had made a good guess. The train had belonged to Gail's father when he was a boy. Every Christmas he set it up around the tree. "For Gail to play with," he would say, even though he spent more time running it than she did.

Tommy ran along the track, full of curiosity. "The wheels run on two tracks, but what's the third rail for? What's that black box for? Why are there wires attached to the track?"

"Hmm. Very strange." Sir Gregory was mystified.

Maribelle peeked around the other side of the black box. "What's this little red thing for?"

Sir Gregory eyed it thoughtfully. "I'm not sure. It looks something like the lever on Abby's old music box."

"Leave it alone, Maribelle!" Lady Alice ordered. "We must hurry."

"Quite right, my dear." Sir Gregory glanced regretfully at the train. He organized everybody quickly. "Lady Alice, as lookout you will please stand by that chair leg where you'll have a good view.

"Maribelle and Tommy, you can help choose the tree." Sir Gregory seized a low-hanging branch. Pulling himself up, he reached down a helping hand to the children. After much crawling around on the branches, they found a small piece that was just right. It was not too tall, not too bushy, and only a little flat on one side.

Sir Gregory settled himself astride the base of the branch. "Stay back," he warned. Grasping the handle of the sword in both hands, he dealt a crashing blow. The branch shook, but the bark was tough, and the sword was not very sharp.

Tommy soon tired of watching his father work, and he swung to the ground. Staying under cover of the branches, he made his way back to the train. He eyed the little tender longingly. "It wouldn't hurt just to sit in it," he told himself.

Meanwhile Maribelle had also climbed down from the tree and sneaked back for another look at the black box.

She was curious about the little red thing. If she moved it, would the box play a tune? Surely a tiny nudge wouldn't hurt.

Maribelle leaned out and put both hands on the lever. Just as she pushed, Sir Gregory yelled, "Tim-m-m-ber!" The cry startled her, and she shoved harder than she had intended. The lever moved easily. She stumbled forward, shoving it all the way.

The train roared to life. Horrified, Maribelle saw it disappear around the bend.

10
Danger!

As the engine leaped forward, Tommy gripped the sides of the tender, but he was more excited than afraid. The wheels raced CLICKETY CLACK, CLICKETY CLACK, and the shining headlight cut a bright path through the shadows. He saw Sir Gregory's legs dangling from the tree. Lady Alice stood at her post, stiff with shock.

Maribelle leaned against the black box. Daringly Tommy let go and waved. She gazed back in awe at what she had done.

CLICKETY CLACK, CLICKETY CLACK. From the cavelike darkness of the next room, two glowing eyes leaped toward Tommy. A numbing fear clutched him. Once before those yellow eyes had stared cruelly down at him.

Around whizzed the train. Maribelle still stood helplessly beside the black box. "The cat! The cat!" shouted Tommy.

Gwib crouched beside the track, and Tommy saw the fur rise on her back. He saw the fierce glare of her yellow eyes and heard her angry hiss. Fright choked Tommy's throat, but Gwib jumped back just as the train passed.

The train! It was the moving train that had aroused the cat. Yet Gwib was afraid of the fierce rushing monster with its one bright eye. The next time around, Gwib was still waiting, a paw outstretched with claws bared to strike. Again her courage failed, and she only clawed the air.

Tommy shivered. If she lost her fear and wrecked the train, he could be smashed into a hundred pieces.

The train sped round and round. Sir Gregory had joined Maribelle. But what could they do? "Go home! Go home!" Tommy shouted bravely as the train rushed by.

Where was Gwib? For a moment Tommy thought she had given up the contest. Then the cat leaped from a nearby chair, landing just short of the tracks. *She's still afraid,* Tommy told himself as he rocketed past.

Now no one was standing beside the black box. Maribelle, Sir Gregory, and Lady Alice had disappeared. Tommy had told them to go, but a lonely feeling swept over him.

A minute later, however, Sir Gregory stood once more beside the track. Tommy felt a swirl of hope.

Around and around raced the train. The cat chased after

it, leaping here and leaping there. It had become a terrible game, with Gwib growing bolder and bolder. Now she stood astride the tracks, feet braced, back arched, the white tip of her tail twitching.

Tommy gripped the tender. *There's going to be a terrible wreck. I'll be smashed to pieces.* At the last possible moment, Gwib leaped aside. *She's afraid, but she won't give up,* he thought in despair.

As the tender raced by, Sir Gregory shouted, "Don't move when I stop the train."

Tommy raised a hand to signal he had heard, but, *How can I escape if I don't run?* he wondered. He felt the train slowing and saw Gwib with her paw raised.

With a mighty swat, the black paw knocked the engine off the track. It lay on its side, wheels spinning in the air. The tender was dragged after it, half-tipped over but still coupled to the passenger cars, which had stayed on the tracks.

Tommy felt as if his head were spinning, too. *A wreck! I've been in a wreck! I've had an adventure like a real explorer,* he thought proudly. He lay still just as Sir Gregory had ordered. A shadow moved above him. Yellow eyes glared down in triumph. If he stayed bone-china still, the cat would leave him alone.

The black head and fierce eyes drew back and disappeared from view, but he dared not move. It seemed a long time before he heard a whisper, "Easy now. I'll help you up. Careful."

Tommy felt giddy with relief as his feet touched the floor. Cautiously he wiggled his china bones. *Nothing broken,* he thought.

"This way," whispered Sir Gregory.

Tommy glanced about and saw Gwib sitting in the dining room. Her back was toward him, and she was tenderly licking a paw.

"Serves her right," growled Tommy. "Would have served her right if she'd smashed her paw flat." Sir Gregory motioned him to follow. Not until they were away from the cat would they be out of danger.

Prompted by Sir Gregory, Maribelle had managed to guide the frightened Lady Alice under and behind the furniture out to the hallway. She had prodded, encouraged, and all but pushed her mother back up the stairs while her father stayed behind.

When at last they arrived at the dollhouse, Maribelle helped her mother into a chair. "Sit down and rest. I'll ask Becky to make you a cup of tea."

Lady Alice sank down. She trembled with anxiety, and

her vapors were in a turmoil. What had happened to Sir Gregory and Tommy?

Sir Gregory had kept his cool. From the moment Gwib leaped out of the dark until he and Tommy pushed and backed their way up the stairs, he had strained every china molecule to save his family.

Tommy had been a brave little boy, thought Sir Gregory as they slipped through the crack into Gail's room. He patted Tommy's shoulder. "Well done, Son."

Tommy grinned up at him. "I guess we outfoxed that old cat." Now that they were safe, Tommy could laugh.

"Right. We outfoxed him—or perhaps we should say we outcatted him." Sir Gregory laughed heartily at his own joke. "We'll make a great pair of explorers, we will." Arm in arm, they swaggered across the room.

At the sound of voices, Lady Alice tottered to the porch. Maribelle and Becky hurried out from the kitchen. They saw Sir Gregory and Tommy laughing as if they had not a care in the world.

Lady Alice's anxiety blazed into anger. While she worried herself sick, those two were strolling home, laughing and joking! But where was the tree? Without so much as a "Thank goodness you're safe," she shouted, "Where is our Christmas tree?"

Sir Gregory stopped short. He had forgotten the tree! His vapors churned. "Don't worry. Tomorrow night . . ."

"Risk our lives again with that cat around? Never! We won't have a tree, and it's all your fault, Sir Gregory."

"My fault!" Sir Gregory was stunned. He had expected to be met with cries of relief and words of praise. Furthermore, it had been Maribelle and Tommy's fault, not his. Still, he should have remembered the tree. *I will have to figure out a way to get it,* he thought, as he sat down at the oak desk in the Sword Room.

Little prickles ran across the back of Sir Gregory's neck. *Wish! We must wish with all our might that Gail will plan a Christmas party.*

11
Aunt Abby Arrives

Gail came straight home from school—home, not to Mrs. Benson's. Yesterday she had gone with Mother to the airport to meet Great-Great-Aunt Abby. She had expected to see a feeble old lady hobble from the plane. To her surprise, Mother hurried forward and greeted a sprightly little lady in a long black sealskin coat and matching fur cap. She scarcely used the silver-headed cane grasped in one hand, and she held her head proudly.

"Forget thee not the Wurling name." The words floated through Gail's mind, and then Mother was introducing her. Gail stared at the round pink cheeks and bright blue eyes framed in a fluff of white hair. Shyly she extended her hand. "I'm glad to meet you, Great-Great-Aunt Abby."

Aunt Abby took her hand. "Oh, my dear, with that red-gold hair, you remind me so much of Corrine." The blue eyes twinkled. "But gracious, just call me Aunt Abby. All those great-greats make me feel old." She tapped the silver-headed cane. "Don't let this fool you. I only carry it to keep people from bumping into me." She smiled, and the corners of her eyes crinkled.

Gail's shyness disappeared. She found herself chattering as easily as she might have with Susan.

"This is my Great Adventure, you know," confided Aunt Abby. "It's my first airplane ride and my first trip west. As a child I imagined all kinds of adventures. Last week I made up my mind that it was high time I had a real one."

Yesterday, Mother and Daddy had wanted to visit with Aunt Abby. This afternoon, thought Gail, she would have Aunt Abby all to herself. She pushed open the front door and was greeted by the delicious odor of fresh-baked cookies.

"That you, Gail?" called Aunt Abby. "Come have a molasses cookie hot from the oven."

Gail sat on the floor in front of the dollhouse, munching her third cookie. Aunt Abby sat beside her on a low stool. "My old bones are getting creaky," she said.

"We haven't fixed up the dollhouse yet," apologized Gail. "Mother's been too busy. Seems like she's always too busy since she went to work for Mr. Easterday."

Aunt Abby's white head nodded. "Of course she's too busy. But you and I have plenty of time. We'll do it ourselves."

"Can we start now?" Gail asked eagerly.

"Now," said Aunt Abby. "Let's begin by pasting up the corners of the wallpaper."

Gail brought a bottle of thin white glue. She squeezed and spread glue, and Aunt Abby's wrinkled hands smoothed the paper into place. Aunt Abby wiped the edges with a rag and eyed the paper critically. "That's better, but what we really need is new wallpaper. The entire house needs redecorating."

"Could we do it for Christmas?" Gail begged.

Aunt Abby laughed. "Christmas is next week. There isn't time."

Before starting to work, Gail had moved the dolls down to the Sword Room. "So you'll be out of the way of the workmen," she explained. Sir Gregory could not see what was happening, but he listened. All the dolls listened. *Wish!* whispered Sir Gregory. *Wish for a Christmas tree.*

Little prickles ran across the back of Gail's neck. She waved a sticky hand. "A Christmas tree! Aunt Abby, maybe the dolls could have a Christmas tree!"

Gail has the gift! I told you so, whispered Sir Gregory.

Aunt Abby nodded at Gail. "Corrine and I always decorated the dollhouse for Christmas."

Christmas in the dollhouse! the dolls whispered to one another. *Christmas in the dollhouse!* Their vapors dipped and swirled.

Aunt Abby smiled happily. "Corrine was eight years older than I. However, she often played with me in the dollhouse. She liked parties with decorations and real food—tiny cookies and cakes and tea in the silver pot. Christmas was the best time of all."

"I know where there's a tree!" exclaimed Gail. "I saw Gwib playing with a piece of broken branch under our tree yesterday. That naughty cat must have played with Daddy's train, too, because the engine was tipped off the track."

"It's been years since the dolls had a Christmas party," Aunt Abby said. "We used to decorate the entire dollhouse with tiny evergreen sprays, red ribbon bows, and candles. We made presents for each of the dolls. Corrine was very clever with needle and thread."

"What did you make?" asked Gail.

"Little trinkets—necklaces and bracelets from beads, a wire hoop for Tommy with a toothpick for a stick, and books. I drew tiny pictures, and Corrine stitched the pages together."

Aunt Abby sat on the low stool, clasping and unclasping her fingers. Beside her Gail basked in a warm glow of contentment. What a wonderful time she and Aunt Abby were going to have giving a party for the dolls!

In the Sword Room the dolls whispered to one another. *A tree! Our Christmas Tea! Just like old times.*

Gail was so excited planning the Christmas Tea that she forgot to ask Aunt Abby about the parchment in the Sword Room. "Keep faith and seek thy fortune here." That night, when Gail was drifting off to sleep, she remembered. "I'll ask Aunt Abby tomorrow," she promised herself.

12
Who Hung the Parchment?

Aunt Abby sat on the low stool, the framed parchment cupped in one hand and a magnifying glass in the other. " 'Build stone by stone, our motto dear. Keep faith and seek thy fortune here,' " she read aloud.

Gail could not hold back her excitement. "Was there ever a fortune hidden in the dollhouse?"

"Not that I remember." Aunt Abby wrinkled her forehead and tried to search backward into the forgotten nooks of memory. "That looks like my father's printing, but I don't remember ever seeing the parchment." She leaned forward. "A fortune is what I need to solve my financial problems."

Gail stared in astonishment. Why, Aunt Abby was rich. Woodcliff Mansion and all those acres—a fortune in real estate, Daddy had said. Gail forgot that it wasn't polite to talk to grown-ups about money. She blurted, "But you don't have to worry about money, Aunt Abby. You're rich!"

Aunt Abby shook her head. "People today don't want a huge old house, and most of the land was sold over the years. I have almost nothing left." She fingered the parchment. "This is just the kind of prank the Captain would have relished."

"Your father?" Gail asked in amazement.

Aunt Abby put down the magnifying glass. "You wouldn't expect a crusty sea captain to be interested in a dollhouse, would you? But my father was. He was about fourteen when he thought of the dollhouse for his sister, Melissa, and he helped the cabinetmaker build it. Melissa was enchanted and loved fixing it up. At first there were few furnishings. Some pieces, like the cast-iron stove, were bought. Others were makeshift. A box turned upside down served as a bed, and a box on a wooden spool made a table."

"Is that the old table in the attic?" Gail asked.

"So it is!" exclaimed Aunt Abby. "The Captain had a special set of knives and a real knack for carving, and gradually he added new pieces of furniture. He made the dining room set of teakwood from India. The master bedroom pieces are mahogany from Africa."

Gail looked admiringly at the carved legs and scroll-backed chairs. "So little and so perfect."

Aunt Abby pointed to a row of plates on the sideboard. "Wherever he sailed, the Captain hunted for dollhouse furnishings. The forget-me-not china came from England. The hand-blown glass is from Italy, and the jade dragons are from China. The ivory elephants, brass bowls, and candlesticks came from India."

Aunt Abby paused. "I remember all these things. Why don't I remember the parchment?"

"Maybe Margot made it," Gail suggested.

"It looks like the Captain's printing," repeated Aunt Abby. "I knew every inch of the dollhouse, every corner and candlestick. When Corrine eloped, I stopped playing in it. Sir Gregory and I still went adventuring, but I didn't play in the dollhouse anymore. Although I might have forgotten some things, I can't believe I would forget the parchment. Margot's old friend, Anne, packed the dollhouse to send to you. I might write to ask her." Aunt Abby handed the parchment back to Gail.

"It's a mystery!" declared Gail.

Aunt Abby clapped her hands. "While we're fixing up the dollhouse, we'll hunt for the fortune."

Gail was thrilled. Aunt Abby had not laughed and said,

"You couldn't hide a fortune in a dollhouse." She had not argued, "You could hardly hide a twenty-dollar gold piece." Gail forgot that Aunt Abby was nearly ninety years old. Abby of long ago had come to play.

Sir Gregory heard Abby and Gail talking as he sat at the oak desk in the Sword Room. His Abby had no money. She needed help. He felt a tingle run down his china backbone. There was something he was supposed to remember when Abby needed help. *What? Who had hung the parchment in the Sword Room? When?* Sir Gregory felt his vapors stir, but no memory bubble floated up.

Every day after school Gail and Aunt Abby worked on the dollhouse. "Treasures can be hidden in the most unlikely places," Aunt Abby confided. She was gluing a broken leg on the wing chair. "No hollow in this leg to hide a fortune in," she said.

Gail cleaned the marble around the parlor fireplace and tried to stick her finger up the chimney, but there was no hole. "The fortune isn't hidden up this chimney. And it's not in the Sword Room fireplace, either," she added. "I tried every stone, and they're all solid as can be."

"The best place to hunt is where most people wouldn't

think of looking." Aunt Abby poked the cotton stuffing back in the sofa. "No fortune hidden here."

Gail rubbed the wood paneling around the marble fireplace with Mother's lemon-oil polish. "No secret panel here," she declared.

The dolls were still in the Sword Room and could not see what was happening, but they guessed. "I like the lemony smell of the furniture polish," approved Becky.

Lady Alice was in a fizz of delight. "Abby and Gail are planning a Christmas Tea!" But then, "Who will come? Who will the guests be?" she asked anxiously.

Sir Gregory roused himself from his musings. "It's always interesting to meet new people, my dear."

"But who?" worried Lady Alice. "At Woodcliff we always invited the dolls from foreign countries."

"Those days are gone," Sir Gregory told her firmly.

"If we don't have guests, there will be more cookies for me," Tommy announced.

"Don't be a pig, Tommy," scolded Maribelle.

"Gail and Abby will invite the guests," said Sir Gregory, and he returned to his own worries. *Why doesn't Abby ask me to help find the fortune? I always helped in the old days, and we always found what we were hunting for.* Once they had followed a trail of clues to the three big rocks where Abby liked to sit. They were hunting for pirates' gold, and Abby carried a little spade. When Sir Gregory pointed with his foot at a likely spot, Abby dug there, and soon they heard the spade clink against metal. Abby unearthed a small tin box which contained a five-dollar gold piece. It was just like the gold piece she had received for her birthday.

Another time they found a wooden box buried at the foot of a huge oak tree. It had contained tiny gold beads, and Corrine sewed them on a dress for Lady Alice. *Oh, that was the life!* Sir Gregory told himself.

Downstairs in Mother's kitchen, Gail was washing the doll dishes painted with tiny blue flowers. Suddenly the same question that Lady Alice was asking in the dollhouse popped into her mind. "Who will come to the Christmas Tea, Aunt Abby?"

Aunt Abby, busy polishing the tiny silver teapot, looked up in surprise. "Your own little dolls, of course. Corrine and I always invited the dolls from foreign countries that the Captain had brought back from his voyages."

Aunt Abby dabbed on more silver polish. "Corrine's favorite was Queen Victoria. There were also Senorita Lolita and Juan Carlos, the bullfighter; the Japanese dolls, Miss Blossom and Miss Cherry; and Memsahib Vidula Mehta from India. Most of the time we kept them in their boxes so they wouldn't get dusty."

Aunt Abby rambled on. She did not notice Gail's worried expression. "My favorite was Katrina, a little wooden Dutch doll. Corrine didn't think she was elegant enough to come to a tea, but I always invited her anyway."

"My Barbie doll is the littlest doll I have, and she's much too big," Gail said.

Aunt Abby set down the teapot. "Why not invite a friend to bring her dollhouse family?"

Gail twisted the blue beads Susan had given her. "I don't have any friends at this school. I'm new, and . . ." She felt a stab of guilt. She had not tried to make friends. She had just felt sorry for herself because she didn't have Susan. "I play with little Betsy Benson after school," Gail ended lamely.

"Maybe my trunk will come," Aunt Abby mumbled.

Gail wasn't listening. Why hadn't she tried harder to make friends? How could they have a party without any guests? Tomorrow was the last day of school before Christmas vacation!

13
Gail Summons Her Courage

Gail sat in the school lunchroom eating a hamburger and listening to the girls around her chatter about Christmas. Usually she wrapped herself in thoughts about Susan, and the other girls had given up trying to talk to her. Today she wanted to join in. She wanted to say, "My Aunt Abby from Boston has come, and we're planning a dollhouse Christmas Tea."

At last there was a break in the buzz of talk. Gail took a deep breath. But before she could say a word, at the other end of the table dark-haired Sharon Kent spoke. "What I want most of all for Christmas is a four-poster bed for my dollhouse."

With a surprised gasp, Gail leaned forward. "Do you

have a dollhouse?" Her words were lost in the babble of the other girls. She tried to catch Sharon's eye. Maybe Sharon could come!

A buzzer rang. Hastily Gail gulped the last bite. If only she could walk with Sharon. No, Sharon had already linked arms with a girl on either side.

Although Gail was shy, she did not give up easily once she had made up her mind. Sharon sat in front of her. The minute they were in their seats, she would ask her. In her heart Gail knew Sharon had tried to be friendly. She always smiled and said "Hi" in the morning. Gail would return a thin little smile and a sober "Hi" and wish Susan were sitting there.

Gail slid into her seat, but Sharon's back was toward her. She was talking to Katie on the other side of the aisle. Gail glanced nervously at the teacher standing in the doorway. Any second Mrs. Hardy would close the door. "Sharon!" hissed Gail, but Sharon did not turn. In desperation, Gail reached across her desk and gently punched Sharon in the back. "Sharon!" she hissed again.

Sharon swiveled in surprise.

"I have a dollhouse," blurted Gail. "A big old dollhouse with a four-poster bed, a silver tea set, jade dragons, and lots of things Captain Wurling found on his voyages."

Sharon stared in amazement. Gail had hardly spoken two words before.

"It isn't all fixed up yet," Gail hurried on, "but we're planning a Christmas Tea next Tuesday. Could you come and bring your dollhouse family?"

"Where do you live?" Sharon asked.

"Only a few blocks from school." From the corner of her eye, Gail saw Mrs. Hardy closing the door. "Oh, please come."

Sharon's friendly face beamed. "I'd love to, if my mother will let me."

Gail tore a piece of paper from her notebook and scribbled her phone number. "Call me tonight," she whispered as Mrs. Hardy rapped for order. Gail sank back in her seat. She had done it. She had invited company to the Christmas Tea.

Now that company was invited, Gail and Aunt Abby worked harder than ever. Aunt Abby held Tommy in her hand, frowning at his ragged, chopped-off hair. "He needs a new wig. Indeed, they all need new wigs."

Aunt Abby hunted through the yellow pages in the telephone book and found a doll repair shop. "Tomorrow is Saturday. Maybe your mother could take us when she does errands."

They washed and ironed, swept and dusted. They made Christmas wreaths from green pipe cleaners and tied on bows of narrow red ribbon. Red birthday candles cut in different lengths decorated the mantel and dining table.

Gail found a magazine page bordered with pictures of red poinsettia plants. She cut the flowers out, glued them to pieces of toothpick, and "potted" them in modeling clay in the brass bowls and in old toothpaste caps turned upside down for pots. There were poinsettias in every room in the house.

A red plastic top from Daddy's shaving cream can and more modeling clay made a stand for the Christmas tree. They decorated it with tinsel and bits of popcorn strung on thread.

Mother gave Gail a pile of old Christmas cards saved from the year before. Aunt Abby cut out a little nativity scene. Gail cut out a gold star and tree ornaments.

It would have been hard to tell who were the most excited— Gail and Aunt Abby or the dollhouse family.

Maribelle twirled around in her new dotted-swiss dress. It was white with red dots, and Gail had tied a red bow in her new smooth yellow curls. "It's the most beautiful tree we ever had," trilled Maribelle.

Tommy chuckled. "Our own tree that we cut down ourselves. Gail thought Gwib did it." He turned a cartwheel that sent his blue trousers flopping about his legs. It was lucky that his new brown wig had been glued on tight.

Lucky, too, that Lady Alice did not see him. She had stopped in front of the hall mirror to admire the glossy brown hair piled high on her head. Her blue silk dress, mended and smelling slightly of cleaning fluid, didn't have a spot on it. She swept into the parlor. "Did you hear? The guests invited to our Christmas Tea are named Kent. Do you suppose the family is any relation to the royal Kents of England?"

"It hardly seems likely," said Sir Gregory, giving his new swallow-tailed coat a tug. Then, seeing Lady Alice's face, he added hastily. "Still, you never know. They could be."

"The Kent children are coming, too," Maribelle said happily. "We've never had children before, except the little Dutch doll who was so bashful she would hardly say a word."

"A boy is coming," boasted Tommy. "A boy named Dick."

"If it is the royal Kents," mused Lady Alice, "I can tell them that I once knew Queen Victoria."

"A big party is a great deal of work," said Becky.

"You don't have to prepare the food," Lady Alice reminded her. She had overheard Gail asking Aunt Abby about food.

"Plaster food doesn't seem right for a party with real company," Gail had said anxiously.

"We always hired a caterer for our Christmas party," Aunt Abby told her.

"A caterer?" asked Gail.

"Yes, someone who makes a business of fixing food for parties." Aunt Abby had lowered her voice to a whisper. "You and I will be the caterers."

Lady Alice looked admiringly at the Christmas greens and candles and a red poinsettia in a brass bowl. She sighed happily. "Our first company since we moved to Indiana."

Becky smoothed her freshly starched apron. "I hope I haven't forgotten how to serve properly."

"You haven't," Sir Gregory assured her. He gave his coat another tug. Since Sir Gregory had painted hair, he had not needed a wig, but Gail had taken him to the doll repair shop anyway. "So he won't feel left out," she told Aunt Abby.

The woman in the doll shop had been very interested and helpful. When Gail told her about the Christmas Tea, she looked at Sir Gregory's moth-eaten clothes with a frown. "I have just the right scraps to make him a new suit," she offered. "If you will leave Sir Gregory with me, I can have it done by Monday noon."

Sir Gregory was pleased to have a new suit even though the coat did feel a mite snug. However, two nights away from home had upset his plan. It was a daring plan, but he had thought it over carefully. Since Abby had not asked him to help her hunt for the fortune, he would do it on his own. Yes, all on his own he would seek the fortune.

14
The Christmas Tea

"My first company in our new house," Gail said. She had quite forgotten her shyness when Sharon telephoned. They chatted about dolls and dollhouses, and as Gail hung up she thought in surprise, "Sharon and I are friends!"

By Tuesday noon everything was ready. Gail looked admiringly at the table. Melissa had crocheted the lace cloth with the scalloped edges long years ago. Gail had fixed the centerpiece—three red candles amid pine needles sprinkled with glitter. The silver tea service and forget-me-not cups and plates were at one end of the table. There were platters of fancy cookies, a bonbon dish filled with candy, and a bowl with nuts (big nuts cut into tiny pieces).

Lady Alice and Sir Gregory and the children waited in the parlor. Baby Winky sat on her new pink blanket on the floor. Becky waited in the hall ready to answer the bell.

Sharon came promptly at two, carrying a box. Gail flung open the door. "Oh, Sharon, I'm so glad you came!"

"I could hardly wait," Sharon told her. "And my dolls are excited, too." She nodded at the box and whispered, "This is their first party away from home."

Aunt Abby was as excited as Gail and Sharon. The three of them were starting up the stairs when the doorbell rang. "Oh, bother!" exclaimed Aunt Abby. "Go ahead. I'll see who it is."

The Kents had arrived. The bell clanged as the boy Dick pulled the bell rope. Becky let them in and with a bob of her white cap withdrew to the kitchen. There was a flurry of introductions, Gail speaking for her dolls and Sharon for hers.

"It's a pleasure to have you here," Gail said in a deep voice for Sir Gregory. Then, in a soft voice for Lady Alice, "Yes, indeed, we're delighted. Do sit down."

Presently they were seated, the grown-ups in one group

and the children in another, all staring curiously. Because dolls must look in whatever direction they have been placed, it is not bad manners for them to stare.

Sir Gregory saw at once that the Kent family was not made of bisque nor of cloth stuffed with cotton. They were molded from a smooth, skin-colored material. Gail had used the word *plastic*. *Are the Kents made of plastic?*

Lady Alice eyed their clothes. Mrs. Kent's green dress hung barely below her knees and exposed her legs all the way down to her shoes. Little Karen's red velveteen dress was so short that it showed her bare knees.

At the sight of those legs, Lady Alice's vapors whirled. *A very daring style.* However, she had often entertained guests dressed in the costumes of their native countries— Japan, India, Spain, England. *It is not surprising that dolls in Indiana dress differently from dolls in Massachusetts.* It did not occur to her that her own dress might be old-fashioned and out of style.

Dick Kent had on long gray trousers, a white shirt, and a red sleeveless pullover sweater. Mr. Kent wore a dark blue suit and a red necktie.

"You have a beautiful home," Mrs. Kent said (Sharon speaking for her).

"How kind of you, Mrs. Kent," replied Lady Alice (Gail

speaking). "We've just moved and haven't had time to re-decorate, but we wanted to have our Christmas Tea, any-way."

"It was so nice of you to invite us," replied Mrs. Kent. "I'm sure we're going to be good friends. Won't you call me Margaret?"

"Thank you, and you must call me Alice." *How very modern,* thought Lady Alice, but she did not really mind.

Gail spoke for Sir Gregory. "What business are you in, Mr. Kent?"

"I teach chemistry at the college," Sharon answered for Mr. Kent.

"I teach at the college also—in the History Department," Gail said for Sir Gregory. He felt his vapors bubble. *So I'm a history teacher. Am I writing a history book?*

The conversation was interrupted by the sound of men's voices and a bumping and thumping on the stairs. "First door to your right," Aunt Abby's voice directed.

"Aunt Abby's trunk has come!" cried Gail. "She's been hoping it would get here before Christmas."

Aunt Abby poked her head in the door. "Go right ahead, girls. I'll be with you in a few minutes."

"Let's wait," said Gail to Sharon. "Aunt Abby mustn't miss the party. I'll show you the rest of the dollhouse. This is the Sword Room. See the swords on the chimney? And listen to this." Gail took the parchment from its nail.

Forget thee not
  The Wurling name,
Nor motto that brings
  Wealth and fame.
Build stone by stone,
  Our motto dear.
Keep faith and seek
  Thy fortune here.

"A fortune? In the dollhouse?" cried Sharon.

Gail nodded. "That's what it says. Aunt Abby and I are hunting for it."

Sir Gregory heard. *Let me help,* he begged.

Aunt Abby rushed in, carrying a box. "Sorry to keep you waiting, but I have a surprise." She settled on her stool, as excited as a little girl.

CLANG, CLANG, CLANG. Someone was pulling the bell rope. Gail gasped at a shimmer of red, gold, and white and hurried Sir Gregory to the door. There was an excited squeal that sounded very much like Gail, then Sir Gregory's voice. "What a wonderful surprise! Please come in. Lady Alice, just see who has come to our Christmas Tea!"

Lady Alice's silk skirts swished. Old friends she had

never expected to see again were crowding into the hall. "Welcome, welcome, dear friends!" she cried.

Queen Victoria stepped forward, dressed in a long white satin gown. A faded scarlet ribbon slanted across her chest, and she wore a golden tiara. "We're delighted to visit you in Indiana."

"Indeed, it's lovely to be here." Senorita Lolita's glossy black china hair was piled high on her head, and the flounces on her red skirt rippled. Beside her, handsome in black knee breeches and a red matador's cape, Juan Carlos, the bull-fighter, gave a courtly bow.

Memsahib Mehta, standing erect and dignified in her red and gold sari, nodded politely. Lady Alice looked enviously at the ruby brooch gleaming on her bosom.

Miss Blossom in a lavender kimono and Miss Cherry in pink clung together. Their sleek black hair was cut in a neat fringe across their foreheads. Slanting black glass eyes shone from delicate white plaster faces with cherry red lips. The wide sleeves of their kimonos fluttered as the Japanese dolls bowed politely.

Last of all, shy Katrina in her wooden shoes, white cap and apron, and faded blue dress peeked from behind the others.

A feeling of joy and gladness filled the air.

As Lady Alice remarked later—much later—they had never had a lovelier Christmas Tea. The refreshments were delicious: wee sugar cookies sprinkled with red sugar or green; little butter-almond strips (Gail had chopped the almonds very fine); tiny pecan balls; chocolate drops the size of a pinhead; slivers of candied orange peel; and nuts. There was even real tea in the silver pot.

"Spiced tea," said Maribelle.

"Plenty of everything," nodded Becky. "Even with unexpected guests and those rascals Tommy and Dick stuffing themselves like pigs, there was still plenty to go around."

While the dolls had their tea, Gail, Sharon, and Aunt Abby had theirs using Gail's own blue willow tea set. They had a plateful of big sugar cookies (trees decorated with green sugar and stars sprinkled with red); little butter-almond strips and pecan balls; raisin-nut chocolate drops and candied orange peel; and hot spiced tea in the blue willow teapot. They chattered over the teacups as happily as three little girls.

Great-Great-Aunt Abby poured a second cup of tea and sipped slowly. The years seemed to circle, shift, and blend. In the timelessness of the dollhouse, the generations mingled . . . Melissa and the boy Vance . . . Corrine and little Abby . . . Margot and her friend, Anne . . . and for a brief mo-

lets, stickpins, and strings of beads—colored glass beads, china beads (the kind used for trade with Indians), and gold-and-silver-colored beads. There was even a necklace with a pendant of tiny pearls.

"Real pearls?" asked Gail.

Aunt Abby nodded. "Lady Alice was proud of her pearl necklace, but from the day she saw Memsahib Mehta's ruby brooch, she wished for a ruby necklace also. And ought to have it, Corrine told the Captain, because it was her birthstone. It happened to be Corrine's birthstone, too."

The second small section held Sir Gregory's black silk top hat and cane, a black silk cravat, a sea captain's hat with gold braid, a battered woolen Scotch cap, and a coil of rope.

"The rope was for climbing," explained Aunt Abby. "We stopped after Sir Gregory broke his leg."

The third and largest section contained an assortment of hats. There was a round sailor hat and two stocking caps for Tommy. A straw hat with a pink ribbon, a red hood, and a white fur cap and muff were Maribelle's.

Lady Alice's hats were the fanciest of all—silk, satin, straw, velvet, and fur trimmed with net, ribbons, flowers, and feathers.

"Corrine loved to make hats," Aunt Abby said. She

picked up a pale blue bonnet trimmed with a bright blue feather. "One of the cats caught a bluejay. It was too late for the poor bird, but Sir Gregory and I picked up a few of the feathers lying about, and Corrine used them."

Mother, overhearing, poked her head in the door. "Yes, my grandmother Corrine had a real flair for making hats. Those first years in Indiana she turned it to good use. My mother told me that the money Grandmother earned making hats and sewing put food on the table."

Aunt Abby stared at Mother. "Corrine made hats and sewed to earn a living? She never wrote that in her letters."

Gail lifted out the tray. The bottom of the trunk was packed with doll clothes—dresses, petticoats, blouses, skirts, capes, jackets, trousers, and shirts. They were made of cotton, calico, linen, wool, silk, satin, and velvet.

One by one Gail handed them to Aunt Abby who mused over them lovingly. Her frail fingers stroked Sir Gregory's exploring suit. The loose-fitting knee pants were streaked with the dirt of long-ago adventures.

"There were no children my age nearby," Aunt Abby recalled. "Sir Gregory was my companion. It's amazing he survived our adventures."

In a bottom corner Gail saw an untidy heap of cotton cloth with a pattern of red, yellow, and black. As she shook it out, she realized that she was holding a doll that had been lying face down.

The sharp, irregular features were whittled from a stick of dark wood. A thin nose crooked slightly to one side above a straight mouth and pointed chin. The doll's scrawny arms hung at her sides, and a red-and-yellow bandana bound up her fuzzy black hair. An ugly brown stain streaked the gathered skirt.

Around her neck a string of glass beads—blue, red, green, amber, and clear—sparkled in the sunlight. Little loops made of glass beads dangled from her ears beneath the bandana.

But it was the eyes that held Gail with creepy fascination. Almond-shaped, they slanted inward. The pupils were bold slashes of white painted from rim to rim across the dark eyeballs.

"Martinique!" Aunt Abby's voice was a hollow whisper. "Martinique, what are you doing here?"

"Martinique?" Gail felt a shiver run down her spine. Maybe it was the spooky eyes. She wanted to let go, but her fingers seemed stuck tight.

"Melissa named her Martinique because she came from the French island of Martinique in the West Indies," said Aunt Abby. "She was the housemaid who cleaned the grates, carried out the ashes, and scrubbed the pots and pans. She was never very popular with the other dolls."

Gail felt a twinge of sympathy. Martinique, too, had been a stranger in a strange place, knowing no one. Gail remembered those awful first days in the new school, the whispers and the snickers.

Aunt Abby gave an apologetic laugh. "Corrine and I seldom played with Martinique. There was something queer about her."

In the dollhouse a whisper trembled from doll to doll. *Martinique! Martinique has come back!*

16
Sir Gregory Remembers

The dollhouse was in a state of upheaval. The dolls had again been moved to the Sword Room, even Winky in her cradle. Gail had piled the upstairs furniture along the tower wall of her room, and she and Daddy had carried the upper part of the dollhouse downstairs.

"It will be easier to work on the kitchen table," Sir Gregory heard Daddy say.

With the upper stories gone, the ground floor had a squatty, chopped-off look. "At least it's a roof over our heads," Becky said cheerfully. For once Lady Alice did not grumble. She had heard Gail and Aunt Abby talking about new wallpaper.

Gail's first idea had been to use the scraps and ends of

rolls left from papering their own house. "But the patterns are too big. They ought to be smaller and more delicate."

Aunt Abby held up a piece left from the Aldriches' living room. "The gold and gray stripes are narrow enough, but the white is too wide."

It was Mother who suggested, "Why not ask Mr. Hawkins at the wallpaper shop for an old sample book, Gail? Daddy has to go to the bank in the morning, and you can ride with him." Schools were still on vacation, and Daddy was writing in his basement study.

Gail had expected Daddy to come into the shop with her the next morning. Instead, he pulled up in front, saying, "Hop out, Gail. You can ask about the wallpaper book while I go to the bank."

"All by myself?" Gail was panicky at the thought of talking to Mr. Hawkins alone. He was a dignified gentleman with bushy gray hair and a large nose. His shaggy gray eyebrows overhung piercing dark eyes.

Daddy tapped the steering wheel impatiently. "After all the business we gave him, Mr. Hawkins ought to be glad to give you an old sample book."

"I don't know him," protested Gail.

"Of course you do. You talked to him when you chose the wallpaper for your room. I'm in a hurry, so scoot."

Frowning, Gail watched Daddy drive away. If she wanted a wallpaper book, she would have to ask for it herself. She hunched her shoulders and pushed open the heavy door.

Rolls of wallpaper pulled down like window shades were displayed along the sides of the store. Tables held piles of sample books. At first Gail thought no one was there. Then a deep voice rumbled, "Is there something I can do for you, little girl?" She saw Mr. Hawkins peering at her from a desk in the back.

Gail stumbled forward. "I—I'm Gail Aldrich," she stammered. "My mother and father bought wallpaper from you."

"I thought you looked familiar." He leaned across the desk. "Do you like the pink roses in your room?"

Gail blinked, surprised that he had remembered. "Oh, the roses are pretty."

"I've always liked roses myself." His mouth turned up in a friendly smile. "Now, my dear, what can I do for you?"

His friendliness gave her courage. "My dollhouse needs new paper. It's a very old dollhouse and all raggedy-taggedy looking because the wallpaper is torn and faded."

Mr. Hawkins cocked his head, his dark eyes bright with interest. "My sister used to have a dollhouse."

"She did?" Suddenly Gail found herself telling Mr. Hawkins all about the dollhouse and Sir Gregory and Lady Alice.

When Daddy honked outside, Mr. Hawkins carried the big sample book to the car. "Don't forget," he said, "when you finish papering, I want to see the dollhouse."

Gail nodded, holding tight to the book. She had made a new friend. That was the second new friend she had made all by herself.

Sir Gregory sat at the oak desk, pen in hand. Gail had said that he was a history professor. *I must be writing a history book,* he thought. *A history of what? Maybe a history of the dollhouse,* he decided at last. *What else do I know so much about?*

Of course, history was full of dates, and he did not have a calendar. *This will be a history without dates,* he decided. Still, it was important to set events down in their proper order.

Tonight Sir Gregory felt distracted by the noise around him. Tommy and Maribelle were racing from one end of the Sword Room to the other. Lady Alice was happily prattling to Becky about the success of their Christmas Tea. Becky, one eye on Winky crawling and squealing on the floor, nodded good-naturedly. It had been her success, too.

Only Martinique sat silent and tight-lipped, staring at the fireplace. She had been very glad to get out of the trunk where she had lain face-down for years. But now that she was back in the dollhouse, she did not feel very welcome. Lady Alice and Becky had almost nothing to say to her. Maribelle and Tommy did not come near. Sir Gregory was busy at the oak desk. Martinique rubbed her skinny hands together. *They'll be sorry.*

One of the first things Martinique had done on her return was to go to the armchair in her room, pull out the cushion, and feel down along the crack. Yes, they were still there— a bead from Lady Alice's dress, a button from Sir Gregory's coat, Maribelle's pink bow, a lock of Tommy's hair, and Becky's dustrag. With a spiteful grunt, she shoved the cushion in place. When she wanted these things, she knew where to find them.

Sir Gregory tapped his pen impatiently and studied the parchment over the mantel. It was an important part of his story. *Who had hung it on the nail? When? Not Melissa.* He was certain of that. *Corrine? Abby? Abby would have asked me to help find the fortune. Help . . . I am supposed to help Abby when she needs it. Who hung the parchment? When?*

Suddenly, as if he felt Martinique's eyes boring into his back, Sir Gregory swung around. "Martinique, do you know who hung the parchment over the mantel?"

The query caught her by surprise. "Not there when Cor-rine stuff Martinique in bottom of trunk."

"So it *was* Corrine who hid you. And right after that—"

"Right after that," Martinique interrupted, "Corrine run away with Timothy O'Leary."

"How do you know? You weren't here!"

"Martinique know," was all she would say.

"That still doesn't tell us who hung the parchment over the mantel and when. You say it wasn't Corrine. It wasn't Abby. After Corrine ran away, Abby never played in the dollhouse. Sometimes she put me in her pocket, and we'd go adventuring. But there were no more parties. Not until Margot and Anne came."

"Margot and Anne!" sniffed Martinique. "Bête comme un chou—as stupid as a cabbage, those two. Find me in trunk and throw me back. 'Grotesque! Queer!' they say." She tossed her head in a huff. The glass bead earrings swayed, making little lights dance on the fireplace stones.

"Margot and Anne spent hours playing in the dollhouse," said Sir Gregory, "but they were the domestic type. The parchment hung right there, and they supposed it was left from Abby's play. They never explored and hunted for treasure the way little Abby did. If Abby had seen the parchment, she would not have left a stone unturned."

Martinique rattled her wooden joints. "Not leave a stone unturned," she mocked. She lapsed into French, and Sir Gregory could not understand a word.

Not a stone unturned. Sir Gregory felt a tingle down his backbone. A memory bubble floated up. He saw the yellow glow of a lantern on the playroom table. He saw the upper part of the dollhouse moved to the floor and felt the lower section lifted. It tilted crazily. The furniture and Sir Gregory slid into a heap in a corner of the Sword Room.

With a thump the ground floor settled onto the table, and the Captain's weather-beaten face peered in. Using the narrow blade of his pocketknife, he poked and scratched around a large stone near the bottom of the fireplace.

Sir Gregory had fallen askew in his chair, but he could see the metal blade chipping and scraping the mortar from around the large pink stone. *What was the Captain doing? Why?*

The Captain's fingers were amazingly nimble, and he soon pried out the stone. He fished something from his pocket, and Sir Gregory caught a peep of leather. *A bag?* His view was blocked by the Captain's broad knuckles as he stuffed it into the space behind the stones. A second object (so small Sir Gregory could not even guess) followed. *What was he hiding? Why?*

The Captain seized the iron kettle from the crane. With a big thumb he wiped the contents (Martinique's painstakingly gathered ingredients) onto the playroom floor. From a pocket he drew a small bottle and a flask. He dumped a gray powder from the bottle into the kettle, added liquid from the flask, and stirred it with his knife.

Scooping some of the moisture onto the point of the blade, he smeared it generously around the edges of the hole. Then he dabbed some on the stone and fitted it back in place. Deftly, he trimmed away the excess mortar. When all was done to his satisfaction, he wiped out the kettle with his pocket handkerchief and cleaned the blade of the knife on his pants.

The Captain was moving the furniture into place when he noticed Sir Gregory slouched in his chair. Sir Gregory's vapors churned wildly as powerful fingers closed around him. Sea-blue eyes stared hard into the glassy gray ones. "You'll not give away our secret, will you, Mate? Swear you'll forget what you've seen this night until Abby needs your help. Swear!"

Outside the dogs began to bark. *I swear,* whispered Sir Gregory as the Captain thrust him into his chair. His vapors swelled with pride. "Our secret until Abby needs your help." Captain Vance was entrusting him with a secret mission!

He was so pleased and excited that he paid no attention when the Captain suddenly swore, "Shiver my timbers! I almost forgot."

Now Sir Gregory recalled being shoved out of the way again. Had he heard a sharp tapping? Was the Captain pounding a nail above the fireplace? At the moment the noise had not seemed important. Had he remembered because Abby needed his help? He must tell her at once.

17
Gail Makes a Trade

The upper stories of the dollhouse stood once more atop the ground floor. There was a smell of fresh paper and paint, and each night the dolls raced upstairs to see what else had been done.

The furniture was not all in place yet, and only a few windows had curtains, but Lady Alice bubbled with excitement. She especially admired the parlor wallpaper: it had pearl gray and gold stripes against oyster white. "Elegant! Truly elegant!"

Martinique eyed it disdainfully. "Dull as cold ashes," she muttered. "Bright colors the *joie de vivre*—the joy of living." But no one ever paid any attention to Martinique.

"It reminds me of the wallpaper in Gail's parlor," said Lady Alice, and she was right. It had been Gail's idea to narrow the white stripes by cutting a few inches off each one. It was Aunt Abby's idea to cover the music room with the same paper.

Lady Alice turned and saw a splash of rich crimson velvet draped over a chair. "How elegant against the wallpaper! Do you suppose this is for the draperies?"

Martinique looked enviously at the crimson velvet. Her wooden joints rattled. She knew very well that not so much as a scrap of anything new would find its way into her room.

Sir Gregory followed Lady Alice from room to room, taking pleasure in her delight. The once dark hallway was now white flecked with gold. The dining room was sunny with yellow flowered paper above the oak wainscot. Sheer white curtains and yellow draperies hung at the windows.

Becky beamed at the apple-green-and-white kitchen. "Fresh as an April day after a shower."

Big as the pages in the sample book were, they were not large enough to paper an entire bedroom. Lady Alice thought Gail and Abby very clever to have chosen a design for one wall and matching plain paper for the other two. A blue-and-gold pattern adorned Sir Gregory and Lady Alice's bedroom. Blue was Lady Alice's favorite color.

Maribelle thought that her room with the pink rosebuds was prettiest of all, but Tommy disagreed. "My clipper ship is best of all," he bragged. The big ship with its white sails filling an entire wall had been Aunt Abby's idea. It had been her idea, too, to paste a piece of matching background over the tip of another boat that showed in one corner. The patch was hardly noticeable unless you knew where to look. Gail had fringed a bright blue bedspread, and Aunt Abby had stitched a red yarn anchor in the middle.

Everyone was happy except Martinique. Her room had not changed and would not, she thought sulkily—not even though her bedspread and curtains had faded to an ugly gray. Early she had cherished a hope for the wallpaper with green and yellow parrots she had glimpsed in the sample book. However, Gail and Aunt Abby preferred to keep the pine paneling in the ground floor rooms.

Martinique's eyes smouldered sullenly. *"Bête comme un chou*—stupid as a cabbage," she grumbled.

Becky kept a troubled silence. Tommy and Maribelle wished Martinique had not come back. She no longer commanded them to run errands for her, but who knew when that skinny hand might beckon?

Sir Gregory kept an eye on Martinique sulking near the stone fireplace. Every day he inspected the kettle to make sure there was not so much as a fuzz of dust in it. He did not believe in voodoo spells, Sir Gregory told himself. Still, he could not explain a faint uneasiness. He was irritated to think that any hocus-pocus might have occurred under his own roof without his knowing about it. He did not intend to let such things happen again.

However, Sir Gregory had a greater worry. How could he tell Abby about the secret hiding place when she would not listen? She chattered to Gail as they worked, or she was preoccupied with her own problems. Gail did not listen, either. It was as if the electric current from a radio transmitter had been turned off.

"I'm glad I didn't know that Queen Victoria and the others were coming," Gail had said to Aunt Abby after the Christmas Tea. "Because if I had, I would never have screwed up my courage to invite Sharon. I did, and now I have a new friend."

When school began again, Gail found that she had lots of new friends. Sharon had told the other girls about Gail's wonderful dollhouse. They clustered about her, begging to come and see it.

Gail felt a warm, happy glow. "I want all of you to come," she said, and her smile included Madge. "I'll have to ask my mother, though, and right now the dollhouse is all torn up. Aunt Abby and I are making new curtains and bedspreads and upholstering furniture."

"Only one visitor at a time," Mother said. "Perhaps one a week while you are so busy fixing up the dollhouse. We mustn't wear Aunt Abby out."

"She likes fixing up the dollhouse," insisted Gail. "She says it makes her feel young again."

"Sometimes I think she is worrying about something," said Mother. "Do you know what it could be, Gail?"

"It might be money," Gail said, remembering.

"Money?" Mother shook her head. "Aunt Abby doesn't have to worry about money."

Gail fingered her blue beads. "She says that's what everyone thinks, but she has almost nothing left. She's poor."

"That's hard to believe," Mother said slowly.

"Look what I have, Aunt Abby," called Gail as she bounded in from school one afternoon. She unfolded a silk scarf gaudy with bright red, yellow, blue, and green. It was square with a design of two large rectangles and two small ones. Each rectangle was outlined with a band of a different color and had stripes of the other three colors in the center.

"What's it for?" Aunt Abby asked.

"For Martinique's room. She likes bright colors, and her bedspread and curtains are so faded and shabby. We can make a bedspread from one big rectangle and cut the other big one in two for the pillowcases. The smaller pieces can be used for the curtains."

Aunt Abby smiled. "It's exactly right for her. Where did you get it?"

"From Jan at school. Her cousin sent it for Christmas. She wore it today with a yellow sweater. I thought of Martinique right off, and at noon I traded Jan my blue beads for it. I promised she could be the next one to come see the dollhouse."

"You traded your blue beads?" Aunt Abby was astonished.

Gail nodded soberly. "I knew I'd never find anything else that would suit Martinique half so well."

Martinique was in a daze. She sat on the red, yellow, blue, and green bedspread. She leaned against the new silk pillowcases and stared at the red, yellow, blue, and green curtains. *Gail make for me*, she whispered. *She make because she know I like. She trade her blue beads!* Never before had anyone been so kind to Martinique. The old spitefulness seemed to melt away. Slowly she walked over to the arm-chair and removed the cushion. Feeling down along the edge, she pulled out a gold bead, a gray button, a pink bow, a wisp of hair, and a dustrag. For a long moment she looked at them. Then she walked to the back of her room and knelt beside a crack between the floorboards. One at a time, she pushed the objects through. She heard the bead and button roll away.

Gail was at school when Sir Gregory heard Abby come slowly into the room. She eased herself down on the stool and plucked Sir Gregory from the Sword Room. She held him in a frail, trembling hand. "The deal fell through, Sir Gregory. I counted on it, and the deal fell through."

She waved a white envelope. "Mr. Scott says he could sell half an acre of my land, but he advises me to wait and sell what's left all in one piece. What do I do for money in the meantime? I can't even buy my plane ticket back to Boston." She shook Sir Gregory in a kind of desperation. "What do I do for money?"

Sir Gregory's vapors spun wildly. Abby needed help. His Abby had come to him. *I know! I know!* he cried.

Abby was so upset that she did not hear. She clutched him tighter and rambled on. "I was ten when Corrine eloped with Tim O'Leary. Nothing was the same after that. Mama sick, Sheldon lost at sea, and the Captain always grim and silent. He was never himself again, and later he did and said such queer things."

Sir Gregory tried once more. *The fortune, Abby. Hunt for the fortune.*

"Fortune!" groaned Abby. "Raving like a madman about a fortune. Made me promise I'd always keep the dollhouse. 'A fortune for little Abby,' he said. By then I was grown."

I saw him hide it, Abby. If you'd only listen . . .

"Listen! I should have listened to Mrs. Harper and sold her the dollhouse."

Abby, the pink granite stone . . .

"The old Gramophone, marble tables, four-poster beds. . . . Mrs. Harper stripped Woodcliff of its lovely old furnishings, and the money paid the taxes, the bills, and the down payment at the retirement home."

Sir Gregory felt as if his china bones would crack with frustration. Abby was only skimming a word or two of what he was trying to tell her. *The verses on the parchment, Abby. They're the clue the Captain left. Think, Abby, think!*

Tears wet the faded roses in old Abby's cheeks. "Think! I no longer know what to think!" With fumbling fingers, she set Sir Gregory in his chair and went away.

18
The Secret of the Sword Room

Sir Gregory's vapors were churning a froth. Abby needed help, but Abby no longer listened. Sir Gregory stared at the papers on the oak desk. *Gail has the gift, but she is too busy fixing up the dollhouse. Somehow we must catch her attention.*

A shining idea bubble floated up, and Sir Gregory sprang to his feet. *It might work! It's worth a try!* He shoved a stool to the fireplace, leaped upon it, and then jumped to the mantel. Balancing himself, he seized a sword.

Lady Alice stared in astonishment. "Sir Gregory, what

are you doing?" All the dolls were staring at him.

"We've got to help Abby," he cried, jumping down.

"Help Abby?" Lady Alice was puzzled.

"Abby's in trouble. She needs our help." He was peering at the fireplace stones. "Hmm. Maybe that's the one." He backed away, studying the stones intently, and then gave a satisfied nod. Clutching the sword with both hands, he stabbed at the mortar around a large stone near the bottom.

"Sir Gregory!" Lady Alice's voice rose in alarm. "Do you want the fireplace to tumble down around us?"

Sir Gregory scratched vigorously, and a trickle of cement powdered the floor. "Don't fuss, my dear. I'm only loosening this one stone."

"Why? What for?" Maribelle and Tommy clamored.

Gray crumbs fell away as Sir Gregory picked and scraped. He glanced at their bewildered faces. He pointed the sword at the parchment. " 'Build stone by stone, our motto dear. Keep faith and seek thy fortune here.' "

"Fortune! Here?" gasped Lady Alice.

"Land sakes!" Becky bounced Winky in her arms. Maribelle and Tommy squealed with excitement. Only Martinique was silent.

"Fortune!" repeated Lady Alice. "What makes you think . . ."

Sir Gregory jabbed harder. "I was here. I saw the Captain pry out this very stone and hide something behind it."

"What did he hide?" shouted Tommy.

Sir Gregory shook his head. "I couldn't see, and the Captain made me swear I'd forget until Abby needed my help. That time has come, but Abby no longer hears me, and Gail is too busy fixing up the house." Sir Gregory slashed his sword through the air. "We must attract their attention!"

"Martinique help," a flat, wooden voice offered unexpectedly.

"You?" Becky's usually mild voice was stern. "What did you ever do besides cause trouble?"

"I not mean to cause trouble," Martinique answered sullenly. "When Abby not around, Corrine talk to herself while she sew. I know she think of running away with Timothy, and I try to stop her. When she finish Lady Alice's dress, she say she make turkey red curtains for my room. No want Corrine to leave until red curtains made."

Lady Alice tapped her foot impatiently. "How could you expect to stop Corrine from running away?"

"Make voodoo spell," Martinique retorted stubbornly. "But time too short. Now Gail so kind to Martinique, I want to help her."

Forget this not
The Wurling name
Nor motto that brings
Wealth and fame
Build stone by stone
Our motto dear
Keep faith and seek
Thy fortune here

Sir Gregory had stuck with his task, and he felt the stone move. He gave another hard jab, and with a final sifting of cement, the great stone lay loose in its socket. "It's free! Gail has only to pull the stone out!" he cried jubilantly.

The afternoon sun was streaming through the tower windows when Aunt Abby came in, carrying the red velvet drapes. Gail had some little nails and a short-handled hammer. "We don't need to wait for Daddy. I can put up the rods myself," Gail declared.

She began to pound, but the blows went wild. They missed the nail and then bent it. She tried a second nail with no better luck and dropped the third one. "Oh, bother!" Leaning down, she saw the sword on the floor. "I pounded so hard that a sword fell down," she told Aunt Abby.

Fortune, fortune, hunt for the fortune. The dolls wished as hard as they could.

As she reached for the sword, Gail saw the gray crumbs and examined them curiously. "My pounding must have jarred some cement loose around the fireplace!"

"The mortar is very old," sighed Aunt Abby.

Abby! groaned Sir Gregory. *The fortune. Hunt for the fortune. Use your imagination*. That was the trouble with grown-ups. Their imaginations dried up from disuse.

Gail was reaching again for the sword when, WH-I-I-I-SH, the parchment fell, nail and all, and landed at her fingertips.

Becky was startled. *Martinique's voodoo worked!*

"Now how did that happen?" Gail complained.

"Well," Aunt Abby said, "you've had that parchment up and down so many times that I expect the nail worked loose."

But Becky knew better.

As Gail reached for the parchment, she felt a prickle across the back of her neck. "Build stone by stone, our motto dear. Keep faith and seek thy fortune here." The prickles scurried faster and faster across her neck.

A beam from the lowering sun sparkled on Martinique's glass beads. A reflected ray shone like a spotlight on the shiny flecks in the big pink stone. Gail stared at the crack around it. As if in a daze, she stretched out a thumb and forefinger. The stone pulled out easily, like a ripe plum waiting to be plucked. The ray of light blinked into a gaping hole.

"Aunt Abby! Oh, Aunt Abby! See what I've found!" Gail pulled out a sandalwood box scarcely half an inch long.

Aunt Abby's chin trembled. "Open it," she said softly.

With a thumbnail Gail flicked up the lid. From a bed of

yellowed satin a tiny red jewel set in gold winked up at them. It was fastened to a fine gold chain, a chain just the right size to slip over a little doll's head. "How sweet!" Gail lifted it out.

"A ruby necklace!" exclaimed Aunt Abby. "I think," she whispered in Gail's ear, "that Sir Gregory asked the Captain to bring a ruby for Lady Alice. She always wanted one, you know."

A ruby necklace for me! Lady Alice's vapors spun dizzily.

"To think," marveled Gail, "that it has been there all these years, waiting to be found."

"So it was a doll fortune the Captain raved about," Aunt Abby murmured.

Look again, Gail, urged Sir Gregory.

Look again! Look again! wished all the dolls.

Gail patted Aunt Abby's shoulder. "I'm sorry there wasn't a real fortune."

"I suppose one shouldn't expect to find a real fortune in a dollhouse," Aunt Abby said regretfully.

Abby, Gail, look again, pleaded Sir Gregory. *There's more. I know there's more.*

More. Look again. Look again, wished all the dolls.

Gail felt the little prickles across the back of her neck. She saw the light shining in the hole and leaned forward.

Her fingers, searching inside, felt a string and touched leather. "Aunt Abby! There is something else! It feels like leather. A little bag maybe."

The bag was not easy to get out. Gail scraped her knuckles on the rough stone as she worked it back and forth. "It went in. It has to come out," she grunted. Bit by bit she eased the bag forward. At last she held in her hand a narrow leather pouch about the size of a man's thumb. The string she had felt was the looped end of a cord threaded through the drawstring top.

"Hold out your hand, Aunt Abby." Gail spread the strings and gave a gentle shake. A glittering hoard spilled into the wrinkled palm. In the midst of a sparkle of diamonds gleamed a red jewel as large as Gail's little fingernail. Its cut surface caught the sunlight and kindled the hidden fire within. Gail stared, speechless.

"A Burma ruby!" gasped Aunt Abby. "Red as pigeon's blood!"

A Burma ruby! cried Lady Alice, her vapors whirling.

Red as pigeon's blood! added Sir Gregory.

A Burma ruby, red as pigeon's blood! echoed the other dolls.

The sun shining through the tower windows cast its rays on the rich brilliance of the ruby until its fiery depths glowed. Gail thought she had never seen anything more beautiful.

There was a catch in Aunt Abby's voice. "The ruby was Corrine's birthstone. Perhaps the Captain planned to have it set in a necklace—and then Corrine eloped."

Gail fingered the leather pouch. "There's something else!" she shouted and drew forth a blue stone that sparkled like the ocean on a sunny day.

"A sapphire! My birthstone." Tears sprang to Aunt Abby's eyes. "I am surprised, though, that the Captain didn't leave a note."

Once more Gail reached into the hole. Her probing fingers drew forth a yellowed paper folded many times. It crackled as Aunt Abby carefully opened the folds, revealing two messages. The first was neatly printed like the parchment. Aunt Abby's voice shook. " 'Cheers for Abby! You have found the ruby necklace and solved the secret of the Sword Room. Faithfully yours, Captain Vance.' "

The second note had been added in a sprawling hand. " 'I write in great haste, for we sail soon. In the recent turmoil, I forgot about Lady Alice's necklace and the other jewels. Your mother agrees with me that there is no safer place to hide them than here. Now you and Sir G. have a real fortune to guard. Do not reveal the secret to anyone else.' "

Tears wet Aunt Abby's cheeks. Gail was crying, too. "Oh, Aunt Abby! Now you won't have to worry anymore about money."

Aunt Abby's gnarled fingers smoothed the creased paper. "The Burma ruby alone must be worth a small fortune now."

"A Burma ruby? What do you mean?" asked a voice. Mother stood in the doorway with Daddy peering over her shoulder.

"Mother! Daddy! There really was a fortune!"

Of course Gail and Aunt Abby had to tell the whole story. How Gail's pounding had knocked down the sword and jarred the mortar loose. (Sir Gregory grinned to himself as he listened.)

How the parchment had fallen when Gail tried to replace the sword. How she had seen a sunbeam reflected on the pink stone. (Now it was Martinique's turn to smile slyly to herself.)

How Gail had pulled out the stone, found the little box and, looking again, felt the string and leather pouch. (All the dolls smiled happily, for hadn't they wished as hard as they could?)

"Well, I declare!" Mother exclaimed in astonishment.

"Well, I never!" Daddy was dumbfounded.

Aunt Abby smiled wistfully. "I was always chattering

about hidden treasures, always pretending, and Sir Gregory was my faithful companion. The Captain always brought back treasures for the dollhouse. As he sailed home on that last voyage, he must have planned the secret hiding place for Lady Alice's necklace—even to printing the verses on the parchment for a clue.

"However, almost from the moment he arrived, he and Corrine argued and quarreled. He was furious when she eloped. A few weeks later, he was getting ready to sail when Mother had her stroke. He wouldn't leave her. Sheldon sailed without him."

"And you no longer played in the dollhouse," Gail remembered.

Aunt Abby nodded sadly. "My happy childhood had ended. My mother died after news came nine months later that my brother Sheldon's ship had gone down in a storm. The Captain brooded over his losses and became even more moody and withdrawn. Luckily for me, Aunt Sadie saw to it that I went to a girls' finishing school there in Boston for several years.

"My poor father never recovered. Gradually, he became more and more confused. I did my best to humor him. If he rushed in calling that he had seen Sheldon's ship sailing into the harbor, I acted happy. If he said Mother would soon be home, I agreed. If he ranted about a hidden fortune, why should I take that any more seriously?"

The tiny necklace with its red eye winked up at Gail. She leaned forward and whispered in Aunt Abby's ear.

"Yes, indeed," agreed Aunt Abby. "And Sir Gregory must give it to her himself."

Aunt Abby tenderly placed the sandalwood box in Sir Gregory's hands. "I have the feeling," she murmured to Gail, "that if it had not been for Sir Gregory, we would never have found the jewels."

Lady Alice sat beside Sir Gregory on the red velvet settee. The ruby necklace glowed on her blue silk dress. She touched Sir Gregory's hand. "To think that my ruby was hidden in the Sword Room all these years."

"If I had guessed what the Captain was hiding, my dear, I should have managed to get it for you long ago."

Maribelle glanced at Martinique. "Queer the parchment tumbled down at just the right moment."

Becky looked at Martinique, too. "Strange that Martinique's beads reflected the sunlight on that big pink stone."

Martinique made no reply, but Tommy said wisely, "You moved, Martinique. Only a bit, but I saw you."

"Gail leave me crooked," answered Martinique. "Can't

help slide." She gave a mysterious little smile. It would not hurt to keep them guessing, but she had the comfortable feeling that at last she belonged.

"We didn't want to move to Indiana," mused Sir Gregory, "but if we hadn't, the jewels would still be hidden." He stood up, his vapors dipping and swirling. "What an exciting history I shall write," he said, and he strode off to the Sword Room.

About the Author

MARJORIE FILLEY STOVER wrote *When the Dolls Woke* for her granddaughter. She has written three other books for children—*Trail Boss in Pigtails, Chad and the Elephant Engine,* and *Patrick and the Great Molasses Explosion*. She lives with her husband in West Lafayette, Indiana.

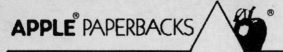

APPLE® PAPERBACKS

Pick an Apple and Polish Off Some Great Reading!

BEST-SELLING APPLE TITLES

☐ MT43944-8 **Afternoon of the Elves** Janet Taylor Lisle $2.75

☐ MT43109-9 **Boys Are Yucko** Anna Grossnickle Hines $2.75

☐ MT43473-X **The Broccoli Tapes** Jan Slepian $2.95

☐ MT42709-1 **Christina's Ghost** Betty Ren Wright $2.75

☐ MT43461-6 **The Dollhouse Murders** Betty Ren Wright $2.75

☐ MT43444-6 **Ghosts Beneath Our Feet** Betty Ren Wright $2.75

☐ MT44351-8 **Help! I'm a Prisoner in the Library** Eth Clifford $2.75

☐ MT44567-7 **Leah's Song** Eth Clifford $2.75

☐ MT43618-X **Me and Katie (The Pest)** Ann M. Martin $2.75

☐ MT41529-8 **My Sister, The Creep** Candice F. Ransom $2.75

☐ MT42883-7 **Sixth Grade Can Really Kill You** Barthe DeClements $2.75

☐ MT40409-1 **Sixth Grade Secrets** Louis Sachar $2.75

☐ MT42882-9 **Sixth Grade Sleepover** Eve Bunting $2.75

☐ MT41732-0 **Too Many Murphys** Colleen O'Shaughnessy McKenna $2.75

Available wherever you buy books, or use this order form.

- -

Scholastic Inc., P.O. Box 7502, 2931 East McCarty Street, Jefferson City, MO 65102

Please send me the books I have checked above. I am enclosing $_____ (please add $2.00 to cover shipping and handling). Send check or money order — no cash or C.O.D.s please.

Name _____

Address _____

City_____ **State/Zip** _____

Please allow four to six weeks for delivery. Offer good in the U.S.A. only. Sorry, mail orders are not available to residents of Canada. Prices subject to change.

APP591

Get ready for fun because you're invited to the...

Bad News Ballet

by Jahnna N. Malcolm

Ballet is *bad news* for McGee, Gwen, Mary Bubnik, Zan, and Rocky! Who would ever think they'd be ballerinas...or the best of friends!

It's the funniest performance ever!

☐ ME41915-3	#1	**The Terrible Tryouts**	$2.50
☐ ME41916-1	#2	**Battle of the Bunheads**	$2.50
☐ ME42474-2	#3	**Stupid Cupids**	$2.75
☐ ME42472-6	#4	**Who Framed Mary Bubnik?**	$2.75
☐ ME42888-8	#5	**Blubberina**	$2.75
☐ ME42889-6	#6	**Save D.A.D.!**	$2.75
☐ ME43395-4	#7	**The King and Us**	$2.75
☐ ME43396-2	#8	**Camp Clodhopper**	$2.75
☐ MF43397-0	#9	**Boo Who?**	$2.75
☐ MF43398-9	#10	**A Dog Named Toe Shoe** (Feb. '91)	$2.75

Available wherever you buy books...or use this order form.

SLEEPOVER FRIENDS™

by Susan Saunders

Available wherever you buy books...or use this order form.

Scholastic Inc. P.O. Box 7502, 2931 E. McCarty Street, Jefferson City, MO 65102

Please send me the books I have checked above. I am enclosing $ _____
(please add $2.00 to cover shipping and handling). Send check or money order—no cash or C.O.D.s please.

Name _____

Address _____

City _____ State/Zip _____

Please allow four to six weeks for delivery. Offer good in U.S.A. only. Sorry, mail orders are not available to residents of Canada. Prices subject to change.   SF1190

APPLE PAPERBACKS

THE GYMNASTS™

by Elizabeth Levy

Available wherever you buy books, or use this order form.

- -

Scholastic Inc., P.O. Box 7502, 2931 East McCarty Street, Jefferson City, MO 65102

Please send me the books I have checked above. I am enclosing $_____ (please add $2.00 to cover shipping and handling). Send check or money order — no cash or C.O.D.s please.

Name _____

Address _____

City _____ State/Zip _____

Please allow four to six weeks for delivery. Offer good in the U.S. only. Sorry, mail orders are not available to residents of Canada. Prices subject to change.

GYM1090